MOON OVER TANGIER

WITHDRAWN

MOON OVER TANGIER

A Francis Bacon Mystery

JANICE LAW

MYSTERIOUSPRESS.COM

OPEN ROAD

.INTEGRATED MEDIA
NEW YORK

Cover design by Mauricio Díaz

ISBN 978-1-4976-4149-5

Published in 2014 by MysteriousPress.com/Open Road Integrated Media, Inc.
345 Hudson Street
New York, NY 10014
www.mysteriouspress.com
www.openroadmedia.com

For Jerry

Francis Bacon was a major twentieth-century British painter, who really did conceive a grand, if ill-advised, passion for an ex-RAF pilot who lived in Tangiers. However, Bacon's adventures in this novel with British spies, Moroccan rebels, KGB men, and forgers, as well as corpses and cops, are purely imaginary and any resemblance there to persons living or dead is truly coincidental.

MOON OVER TANGIER

CHAPTER ONE

A black night in Berkshire. Make that a black, cold, rainy night in the deepest, darkest countryside, a place of distant, unreliable lights; dozing animals; brambles; weeds; thistles. I hate the country, full of bad, youthful memories and things that attack my asthma and empty of all I love: the city, the bustle, the crowds, pretty boys, and rough trade.

Maybe scratch the latter, because I am bruised and bleeding and out in the mud wearing my fishnet stockings and not much else. A bad, mad night that, like so many with David, started well, started excitingly, reached certain dark, ecstatic heights before a deeper darkness, an explosion of real violence, a crazed attack.

You know me: a little pain adds spice to sex. Yes, indeed. But there's a line, and a screaming man armed with lamps and heavy ashtrays and the contents of the cutlery drawer has not just stepped, but leaped, over it. His left hand is at my throat and his right holds a knife. I kick him in the balls and run, gasping in the damp country air full of pollen, hay dust, and animal hair, out into the night. I'm just lucky he didn't keep his service revolver. Because I could be dead now.

There's a faint light behind me: the door I didn't stop to close. David will be a black shape against the light, his voice high and keening so that beyond bruises and cuts, I feel a discrete moment of pain. I know that he's gone far back, back to the war, back to his cockpit with who-knows-what wrong with an engine, flak everywhere, and a Messerschmitt coming out of the sun. A dangerous time and place.

I find my way through the cold and wet to wait out storms of both external and internal weather in the dilapidated cowshed. I don't summon the constabulary or even our neighbor, a farmer whose tastes are more advanced than I'd expected. I sit and shiver and ache, because I love David, because that's the curse of my present existence. I've found I can't live without him, even though, in certain states of mind, he beats me up, and since he hates my paintings, slashes as many as he can get his hands on.

A crazy situation, of course, and totally unprofitable. If my dear Nan were still alive, she'd have a thing or two to say. "Dear boy, stick to Mayfair!" That's what she used to tell me, back in the old days when we were on our uppers and I was an expensive "gentleman's gentleman." But even her heart, so large and resilient where I was concerned, gave out. A gradual decline ended one night while I was away in Monte Carlo, happily losing money playing roulette. A bellboy put the telegram in my hand, and I stepped off the solid and familiar world that Nan had always anchored for me into the abyss, where I found David—witty, handsome, talented, cruel. My beau ideal. Really.

Sometime in the wee hours that night, the lights went out, and I made my way through the mud to the house. He'd locked me out, but I'd hidden a key: I was besotted but not stupid. The next morning, I packed my kit, rescued a couple of canvases, and summoned a cab. Now David was sweet, now he was pleading, but my face was set. My old nanny would have been proud of my resolve, my chilly courtesy, my restraint. I was London-bound with my head churning with ideas and my fingers itching for the paintbrush. A free man, so to speak.

But a week, two weeks, a month later, I would spot him in the Gargoyle, his blond head reflected in the mirrors in the bar, and my heart would stop and then restart to hammer in my ears. The old Greeks were right: love is a recipe for disaster. Next thing I knew, we'd be cruising around Soho, drinking champagne at the Europa, even, folly unto madness, boarding the train at Waterloo for another edition of disaster in the country.

In between times, I painted, enjoying the pleasant illusion of freedom and independence, until, despite all my resolutions, I ventured out to David's usual haunts and allowed myself to be drawn in by his looks, his charm, his wit, his talent, all the qualities that comprised the other side of violence running to cruelty and flirting with madness.

He was funny; he knew interesting things; he played the piano in a way that, even tone deaf as I am, I recognized as brilliant. He'd been brave, too, one of the few who'd patrolled the skies for us and taken terrible losses and flown until they were shot down. That gave him a kind of aura. He'd had what most of us haven't: a moment of greatness. But he'd purchased it at a fantastic price and he was still paying the installments.

There was something else, even more subtle and tormenting: David liked me but he didn't love me. I was too old for his tastes, really, my youthful looks having deceived him. We drank and fought; I left him and came back; I found his indifference intolerable—and irresistible.

After my night in the cowshed, I held out for six weeks. David went off to Tangier, that paradise of slim, dark boys, lacking money or women. Silence for a time, then he sent me a telegram inviting me, asking me, virtually begging me to visit. Doubtless some beach boy had broken his heart; people who've never been down on their luck rarely appreciate the commercial aspects of the sex trade.

I could feel that he was sad, and I was tempted, although I'd promised my gallery new paintings for a show, and I was behind on my work. Virtue prevailed for a while, but when my landlord announced that he was driving from London to Tangier and invited me along, I took it as an omen. Soon we were aboard a Spanish ferry, and the ancient white city loomed against the brilliant African sky and the deeper indigo of the Mediterranean. The stark terraces, blinding and dreamlike in the sun, climbed the hill above the port in fantastic white tiers, and we entered the medina like brides in a white Rolls-Royce.

The crystalline beauty of the city dissolved almost at once. On closer acquaintance, the buildings were battered and in lousy repair; the people, thin and worn; the alleys filthy; the drains stinking. The city had a powerful odor, yet my lungs loved the dry air, and once we climbed the Mountain, the fancy home of the international community, a refreshing breeze came in from the sea.

Palms and eucalyptus and brilliant red and purple blossoms: the Riviera in Africa with much the same mix of remittance men and gangsters, financiers and smugglers, thieves and pedophiles. Lusty young queers rubbed elbows with society types, old North Africa hands, decayed military men, artists, and writers, and even an heiress with jewels as big as pigeons' eggs.

Down below in the Arab town were the folk they'd come for, the hard-working Moroccans cheap to hire for kitchens and gardens. The pièce de résistance was the corps of pretty boys who swanned along the beachfront or lived in the brothels or haunted the alley-ways. Women, too, if your taste ran that way, though that was strictly behind closed doors. Except for the market women in from the countryside, sturdy lasses with huge straw hats, selling vege-tables and grain out of kiosks no bigger than a London mailbox, most native ladies of Tangier were veiled and sometimes hidden.

There were some new people afoot, too: political locals eager to chuck out the International Committee of Control and take over the show. Naturally, Moroccan politics was a closed book to me; I have no time for politics, not even our own. Just the same, living as we did on the interesting borderline between the Mountain and the medina, convenient for the delights of both, we got little hints.

One night in David's rental, a rather pretty one with a roof deck looking toward the sea, I heard shouting in the street: *"Nazarenes, Nazarenes!"* with the thump of a rock, then another, before running feet.

"What was that all about?" I asked him.

"They hate the Christians," he said. "*Nazarenes.* That's us, Chris-tians."

I was struck by the ancient term.

"That's nothing," he said. "Foreigners here are *Roumis*, Romans. They have a long memory."

I might well have considered that, but at the moment I was happy. David was charming, amusing, the way I remembered him best. I'm an early riser, and in the mornings, I sometimes lingered to watch him sleep. He was still quite beautiful then, slim and tanned from the sun with a little red on his shoulders where he had burned at the beach. His hair was bleached nearly white, and his face was unguarded, quiet, and kind. In those hours, I saw the man he had been before the war—intact, charming, talented, brave.

I memorized that face.

Other times I went straight to the flat I'd rented for a studio—and as a bolt hole against romantic storms. Sometimes I tried to paint his portrait, and sometimes I worked on my latest series, paintings of popes in red and purple robes inspired by Velásquez's *Innocent X*, the greatest of all portraits. I love the picture, and more, I love the way it suggests images to me, images of screaming, shouting men looming against darkness. Yes!

Sad to say, Tangier's brilliant sea-reflected light was not conducive to such painting. In fact, travel is not conducive to my painting, period. I always travel with intentions of being inspired and working hard. Usually the work comes to nothing. Delacroix loved the African light, so did Matisse, so did a list of Victorians as long as your arm, but it's not for me. At the moment, I am a painter of shadows and suggestion and violence.

Dark backgrounds, such as I need for my *Popes*, flatten out here. They look like chalkboards and suck away all inspiration. I am a London painter, first to last, and though everything was lovely at the moment, David would ensure that even a successful canvas might not survive. Sooner or later, some bad, mad, possibly wonderful night, I could expect to hear ripping canvas and cracking stretchers.

You see how I colluded in my own destruction. Although pessimistic in the long run, I am an optimist in daily life. Might as well be, given life is absurd. So we walked on the beach, and David picked up boys who would disappoint him, while I gave some painting lessons—and other things—to a charming young Moroccan. We prowled the cafes of the nighttime Petit Socco and met respectable folk at the Palace Bar in the European sector, and everyone else at the Meridian, where David delighted the house by playing the piano. He sang a little, sometimes, in a light, tuneful baritone and exchanged banter with the regulars and winked at me when he began improvising off some popular ditty.

I was happy, yet there was a shadow over the city and over David. While I consumed that wholesome tipple, champagne, he'd gone heavily into spirits, and he was beginning to lose the military smartness and toughness I'd so admired. He smacked beach boys and got beaten for his pains, and wept about their infidelities. Though I could not bear to admit it, I began to pity him.

But things did not start to unravel until one night when we were coming back through the medina very late. I think we were near the police station—our geography at that moment being uncertain—when we heard a groan and a soft scuffling sound.

David gave a wolfish grin, but this wasn't some furtive coupling. Intense events leave deep tracks in memory. My days as an ARP warden during the Blitz had left me alert to damage and ready to act: *locate the victims, stop the bleeding, summon the required emergency services.* Certain sounds bring back the smell of powdered stone and incinerated wood, of leaking gas mains and mud and all the darker smells of violated human bodies.

"Over here," I said. A pale, grayish form, a djellaba-clad body with bare feet. But no boy. A thin, bearded face, a hawk nose, bruised and bleeding cheeks. When I touched his back, trying to help him up, he screamed.

"Hospital? *L'hopitale?*" Most natives had either some French or Spanish.

Though he could barely speak, he was very definite. "*Non, non!*"

"*Gendarmes?*"

"*C'est ils qui sont fait.*"

That decided it. "Find a taxi, David."

"And take him to the house? He could cut our throats. He'll be one of the stone-throwing Istiqlal, wild men out of the Rif. Leave him."

His voice was abrupt, military, a relic of command, but the war

9

had left me with my own imperatives. "Get a taxi now," I said. "He can come to the studio. He's in shock, probably concussed."

I must have hit the right tone, because David went out to the edge of the Socco, where he found a cab and, more surprising, a driver willing to take the injured man in his vehicle. Between us, we got him into the car, although David insisted on getting out at his place.

When we reached the studio, I told the cabbie that I needed help. "I'll pay you," I said, the magic words of the city.

"Not important if you keep him safe."

I took a good look at the man: another thin, bronzed face, wild beard, black eyes. A Berber from the mountains like the injured man?

"Yes," I said.

"Nadir is a good man," he said.

We half-carried, half-dragged his now semiconscious friend upstairs to my studio.

"He needs a doctor," I said after we had settled him on the little divan and I'd brought water and seen the state of his back.

"Too dangerous. Lucky they didn't kill him."

I nodded. I'd heard some things about the Tangier police; plus, I have a deep suspicion of all local constabularies, who either want to arrest me or co-opt me. "We need bandages, salve, disinfectant."

"Give me money and I will get." He was tall for a Berber and the single bulb in the ceiling threw deep shadows over his hooded eyes and under his thin, aquiline nose. Patriot? Thug? Police informer? The wee hours throw up so many possibilities.

"Right." I gave him some dirhams and told him what we'd need, mentally bidding both money and him farewell. I cleaned the injured man as best I could, rid him of his filthy djellaba, wrapped him in a blanket, and had him pee in my turpentine bucket. I was glad to see no sign of blood.

I left his wounds bare in hopes of bandages, and I was brewing mint tea for him when the cab driver entered with two small packages. One held bandages and the other iodine and a local salve that, from the smell of it, seemed potent enough to either kill or cure our patient.

Between us, we painted the injured man's back with iodine, a painful business. We bandaged him up, treated the cuts on his face with salve, and got some hot liquid into him. Bandaged and warm and propped up on the divan, he was able to speak briefly to the cab driver in his own language.

I repeated my concerns about a doctor. "He may have broken ribs or some internal injury."

The cabbie nodded. "First, he must leave the city."

I could only agree.

"No chance tonight. They will be watching all the roads." He gave me a reproachful glance as if I should have known this, as if I should be conversant with the local gendarmerie.

I find it amazing how often innocent gestures on my part involve the police. The offer of a little first aid had slid into hiding a badly injured man, who was important enough, or dangerous enough, to attract police surveillance, maybe even roadblocks.

"Tomorrow?" I suggested hopefully.

"Perhaps. It will take time to arrange. Nadir is a good man," he repeated.

I could only hope so.

I slept on the floor and rose at dawn to check my patient. No more cold sweat—nice regular breathing. All good. When the market opened, I went out for bread and oranges. Nadir ate a little of each, drank more tea, and fell back to sleep, while I struggled to work without much success. Life in the white city, though easy, was proving to have many distractions.

I'd expected someone to collect my patient soon, but when noon came and went, I told him that I would have to go out. "Friends will miss me," I told him in slow, easy French. "I don't want them to come to the studio."

"Good," he said.

I showed him how to lock and unlock the door from the inside and went out to the souk. David was in a cafe, flirting with a pretty brown boy with curly black hair. "How's the Good Samaritan?" he called.

"Can't claim any credit. Cabbie handled everything," I said, lying without hesitation. Later, I was aware that this was another little break between us, but at the moment I just hoped for the right tone, and I guess it was, because David asked if I wanted to see a film or go to the beach.

"Lunch first, then we'll see."

I picked a good restaurant, and by the end of the salads and couscous and lamb with prunes and apricots, David and his new pal were on such excellent terms that I was superfluous. Normally I would have been half-sick with jealousy, but context is everything, and I was relieved. I cruised through the Petit Socco, full of the sort of low haunts I like, then doubled back to the market for a few purchases, including more bread and a handful of dates. I was returning to my studio when a man touched my back. He spoke French, badly but intelligibly, and said, "I have a knife. Don't turn around."

Police? I didn't think so. Enemy of my patient? Possible but unlikely. His rescuer? We live in hope.

I expressed the opinion that he had made an error.

He disagreed and told me to walk straight to my studio. I thought it was best to do that and tried to remember how much I like masterful men. Down the narrow street, through the court-yard, and up the stairs. I rattled the door to alert Nadir, juggled my bundles, and turned the key in the lock. I stepped inside. Nadir was propped up on the bed, and the man behind me, revealed as wiry and dark with one blue clouded eye, pushed past me with a burst of Tamazight and grasped Nadir's hands.

"Issam!" my patient exclaimed.

"He is safe," the stranger said, his face radiant with sudden relief.

"Certainly, but he needs a doctor, and he cannot stay here much longer."

I put out the bread and dates and opened my bundle for the European-style pants, shirt, and sandals I'd bought in the souk, along with a now rather squashed straw hat and a pair of cheap sunglasses.

There was some resistance to my idea, but I displayed Nadir's discarded djellaba, which was badly stained and torn. "He will be a Spaniard, an invalid, and you will be his assistant," I told them. "You can take Nadir's own clothes with him."

We had a struggle to get Nadir dressed. I think only then did Issam realize quite how badly he had been injured. But when we got to the hat and sunglasses, we discovered a further problem: Nadir's face was black across both cheekbones.

Fortunately, I had a solution. I quite like makeup, and living around David I have sometimes needed it. A little foundation, a little rouge, a little dry ochre pigment and Nadir's face would pass muster even if the man himself could scarcely stand.

"A safe place soonest," I said, "and change his dressings twice a day. I had no sulfa powder for him."

"Understood. I will get a taxi."

Nadir and I sat waiting for Issam's return. I saw that his skin was gray under the makeup, and he was silent for a while, as if recovering from the effort of getting dressed. Then he began fiddling with the bracelet around his wrist. The beads were metal with a curious design. He removed one before retying the bracelet and putting it back on. He held out the bead to me.

"This with my name," he said in his hoarse voice, "will keep you safe."

Shades of *The Desert Song* and schoolboy annuals! I was touched, nonetheless. Although I could not imagine being at the mercy of mountain tribesmen, I put the bead in my pocket. At that moment, I much underestimated the weird complexities of life in Tangier.

A few minutes later, Issam returned, and we managed to get Nadir downstairs to the waiting cab—with the useful driver from the previous night. After I tidied away the discarded dressings, I left for the afternoon with a light heart. I met David for dinner, and after a few drinks at the Palace Bar, set off for an evening with the International Zone's high society, presided over by a nice old queen with a big house and a bigger entertainment budget.

Fugitives in the morning, dinner jackets at night. Just the sort of contrast I like, and I could almost hear myself telling David, *My dear, he was too much. Right out of the Rif Mountains complete with dagger, etc.*, as I do love to camp it up. But I didn't say a word about Nadir and his one-eyed bodyguard. On our way to the party, I realized that I wasn't going to say anything to David, that at some level, I no longer trusted him. And that made me sad.

CHAPTER TWO

Up the Mountain in the velvet night. Sea breeze and distant lights; palms and eucalyptus and some heavy-scented flowers that played up my asthma. Still, picturesque. I could imagine old Matisse reaching for his brush and dreaming of orange and green and purple patterns. Not my cup of tea, but I do like luxury as well as squalor, and this promised to be a party deluxe. Our host was a younger son with a handsome allowance from a textile fortune. That, plus an exaggerated fear of prosecution and disgrace back home, had brought him to the International Zone where he enjoyed discreet liaisons and a spectacular garden.

Most of the expats and visitors were present: holiday-making gangsters rubbed elbows with the foreign consuls and legation staffs; poets and musicians, queer to a man, chatted to shady financiers; and society dames with parrots on their shoulders and diamonds in their hair considered propositions from oily types with their eyes on the main chance. Jews who had escaped with two suitcases kept a wary eye on notorious collaborators visiting Africa for their post-Reich health, while big-time smugglers and currency traders exchanged gossip and tried to catch the political winds. It was Monte Carlo with minarets and very much to my liking.

There was a sprinkling of wealthy Moroccans, too, uncomfortable individuals of sophisticated tastes and haughty expressions, and the Zone's new police commissioner, an Algerian import supposedly charged with making Tangier respectable. I, myself, rather enjoy the frisson of illegality, but every other queer in town seemed nervous about the new cop.

I would discover that a number of my compatriots were already angling to get on his good side by fingering others. I had doubts about his success, given the economy of the city, and even though I intended to give him a wide berth, I could not help glancing occasionally at the commissioner. You know painters by their production. Policemen, too, and I'd been overly close to his squad's handiwork.

David took another tack. We'd been drinking and chatting with friends, and he was standing companionably with his hand on my shoulder, fending off (for the moment) requests to "favor us with a tune." He seemed relaxed and content, the latest faithless boy forgotten, my company cherished, and his alcohol intake at a happy level.

I stepped to one side, the better to hear a poet who'd recently had a scandalous success among the easily shocked Yanks. A few moments later, I noticed that David had left our circle. Whether by accident or design, he'd struck up a conversation with the new commissioner, and I could see he was being charming.

That was a conversation I had no wish to join. I have a habit of speaking my mind, especially after numerous visits from the champagne trays. With rare common sense, I sidled to the back of the house, where I began chatting with one of the formidable grande dames of the Zone. Born and raised in Tangier, Miss Woodward was a spinster with a bold profile, Edwardian manners, and something cynical and knowing in her expression that reminded me painfully of Nan. I wasn't sorry when we were interrupted.

"Francis!" This was our host, pale, slightly portly, with an expensive blond toupee and a vague, distracted air that might also be ersatz. Richard was reputed to be a kindly man, except when scrambling up the social ladder of the International Zone. I found him pleasant, but I didn't trust him, perhaps because he always played the old duffer although he couldn't have been even ten years my senior.

"Marvelous party, Richard. The South of France couldn't put on its equal."

He gave a little shiver of pleasure, as if fluffing invisible feathers. "A good party is like a good sherry; it needs a fine blend, I do believe."

"This one has a fine bouquet," I said.

Maybe I laid it on too thick, for he beamed and, leaning over confidentially, said, "I've a favor to ask of you. Bought a little picture a while back. A Picasso, don't you know, and I wonder if you'd take a look at it."

I said that would be a pleasure, a certain period of the Spaniard's work having been a big influence early in my career.

"Splendid. You're just the man I need."

I winked, he smirked; we proceeded down the hall toward the garden. The painting, nicely framed and well lit, was hanging over a fine chest. I saw right away that it was from Picasso's "bone period," a beach scene with a woman, part African mask, part stylized biomorph, sitting at the edge of the water. I leaned in close to the work: the design was handsome, the muted colors lovely.

"Very nice," I said. "Lovely, in fact. Too bad it's a fake."

"Really?"

"The varnish is barely dry," I said. "And look here: the paint layer is so smooth. No pentimento, no indication of second thoughts. Too perfect in a word. I'd guess it's a copy of a genuine Picasso. Probably the image was projected onto canvas, the lines traced, and the paint filled in. With the help of an optical device, anyone with a steady hand could have made it."

I expected Richard would be distressed that his connoisseur's eye had let him down, but though he remarked, "A good bargain is sometimes a bad bargain," there was something curiously avid in his expression. "A moment, Francis," he said, and he plunged into the crowd, returning a moment later with a short, swarthy Algerian *colon*. He had large, almost unblinking eyes that—with his chilly, impassive face—gave him the air of a dangerous amphibian.

"Police Commissioner Bellefleur," Richard announced, and before I had even the thought of escape, I was introduced and found myself shaking hands with the uniformed and beribboned nemesis of my tribe.

"Explain to the commissioner what you just told me," Richard said.

I said that the painting was a copy if not an outright fake. "Naturally, we don't know the intentions of the painter."

The commissioner seemed uninterested in intentionality, for he made an impatient gesture. I guessed he was more of an "eye for an eye and tooth for a tooth" man.

After I pointed out the pertinent details of the canvas, he asked whether the copyist would have needed the original.

"Not necessarily. A good color reproduction would do. If he had the dimensions."

"Explain that," he said abruptly. He was not exactly your society conversationalist. Though his voice was soft and his expression bland, he seemed habituated to command and accustomed to being feared. A taste of mine on certain occasions, but not this one.

"If one knew the size and the colors, the safest painting to forge would be a reproduction of a work lost in the war, because there would be no possibility of comparison."

The commissioner fixed me with his unblinking stare. "I believe you are a painter, yourself, monsieur."

I nodded.

"Who works from photographs. Is that correct?"

I didn't like the way this was going, and I wondered who had been so informative. "Sometimes, yes. But for me, a photograph is just a jumping-off point. This painter"—I gestured toward the fake Picasso—"is set to deceive."

The commissioner shook his head. "No, monsieur, this painter is dead." He frowned and drew himself up and turned to Richard. "We cannot speak further here. Bring Monsieur Francis with you to my office. Eleven tomorrow." And with a curt *bon nuit*, he exited through the garden.

Talk about going from bad to worse—or, as Nan used to say, from the frying pan into the fire. I had no intention of going anywhere near the police station, and I was making that very clear to Richard, when he took my arm and began shaking his head.

"Francis, Francis!" he said. "Think a minute. Think of your situation. Our situation."

"My situation is that I can be on the ferry to Gibraltar any day of the week."

"But not all of us are so fortunate, dear. Some of us have cast our fate permanently in Tangier."

"Where the police appear to spend their time beating up the natives." This was indiscreet, and I reminded myself to avoid any mention of Berbers, particularly political Berbers.

"The police are changing," Richard said. "The Moroccans want their king back, and if the demonstrations and violence continue across the country, you'll see the French will have to bring him home. And really, Francis, Madagascar, for a man of the desert! I don't know what the Frenchies were thinking."

"I suspect they wanted him well out of the way."

"And when he comes back—"

"If he comes back—"

"The Zone will be finished within a year. Mark my words. The new commissioner is already a bow to Moroccan sentiment."

"Another reason not to meet him."

"And you don't have to. You can take the ferry any day, but David is in jeopardy." Richard tipped his head to one side and gave me a sly glance. "Wasn't there an incident the last time you visited? A little altercation in a taxi ending in the local lockup? Blood and bruises sufficient to alarm one of our not easily spooked cabbies?"

"I didn't press charges," I said quickly. I would just as soon have passed over that disastrous and humiliating night, a ghastly combination of jealousy and drink.

"Of course you didn't, but there have been other little incidents with the beach boys. Yes, yes, my dear, I know that he's usually gotten the worst of it, but still. There's a new Tangier around the corner. A bloody great looming disaster, and it behooves us all to be good citizens at the moment."

So, though I am usually immune to appeals for civic duty, I was waiting outside my studio the next morning when Richard appeared with his driver. We arrived in the best Mountain style at the commissioner's HQ, a fine old Moroccan building well beyond the stink of the much less salubrious prison. We were ushered into a handsome tiled courtyard, complete with a small fountain splashing in the morning shadows, and then into a high-shuttered room, where the commissioner sat in state like a minor pasha behind an antique desk with several telephones and an octopus of wires and cords. Behind him were rows of green file cabinets and a large-scale map of Tangier. In front of the desk, three straight chairs awaited unlucky visitors.

"Ah, Richard. How very kind of you to bring Monsieur Francis. I wish all Tangierinos were as public spirited."

He rose from his desk and shook hands, all bonhomie, but when Richard moved toward one of the chairs, the commissioner stopped him. "No, do not trouble yourself, Richard. I will not keep a man as busy as you unnecessarily. There is no need for you to be concerned with sordid police matters." And with surprising deftness, he escorted Richard from the office.

A moment later, he returned, closing the door behind him with a crisp little click like a sprung trap. His manner had changed, too. Richard got the fussy courtesy. I got the stony stare and the big silence. The commissioner sat down and ruffled through some folders before passing a large black-and-white photo across the desk to me.

It was a crime scene, stark in the police flash that spotted the bare wall and the tile floor with reflected light then sank darkly into a slim figure lying facedown. For a moment I could not tell if the corpse was male or female, given the short, thick hair, the capri pants, the sandals. What was unmistakable was the black pool of blood underneath the body.

"A young Spaniard," the commissioner said after I had studied the image. "We think he was the painter."

"Why?"

"He worked for a photographer, a man who produces special images for special tastes and still tints his pictures by hand." The commissioner's mouth gave a subtle twist to indicate disgust; pornographers as well as queers had better watch their step in the newer edition of Tangier. "I am told that work was done with dyes and watercolors. But when we found the body, the boy had traces of oil paint on his hands and on his clothes."

"Did you find any paintings? Prepared canvases?"

"Unfortunately, no. And no device such as you so helpfully described."

I shrugged. "The killer would have been foolish to leave the evidence behind."

"Exactly. There is someone clever behind this."

"A challenge for the department," I agreed.

"Requiring the assistance of civic-minded residents." Though scarcely prepossessing, the commissioner had a powerful presence. I felt his gaze like a sandbag on my chest. He wanted something, and I sensed it would involve me in something unpleasant. *Be careful, Francis!*

"The perpetrators of this scheme will be on the lookout for a replacement," the commissioner said after a moment. "Someone skilled."

"Or semiskilled," I suggested. I thought briefly of the young Moroccan I'd been tutoring. His name was on the tip of my tongue before my better nature whispered that he would be exceedingly vulnerable.

"A man," the commissioner continued relentlessly, "who can recognize a Picasso if it presents itself. Monsieur Richard, with a fine sense of civic responsibility, came to me about the painting. And told me where he'd bought it. I would like you to contact the gallery."

"I already have a gallery in London. My dealer would not be pleased if I open negotiations with a little establishment here."

"My dear monsieur," he said, his voice softened even if his gaze stayed malevolent, "you are clearly an intelligent man. Think of something. Some interest in his pictures, a need for some painting material, or that old reliable: a desire for ready cash. I'm sure you'll think of something."

"I am sure I will not," I said. "I've assisted you enough already."

He said nothing for a moment. Then he produced another piece of paper from the pile and handed it to me. It was an arrest warrant for David. My heart jumped, which was clearly what he'd been counting on, because on closer examination, I saw that there was neither date nor victim.

"This warrant is useless," I said. "No date. No complaint."

"It is in reserve," the commissioner said evenly. "If you help us, it remains blank. If not, I can find someone to complain within the hour. Be assured of that, Monsieur Francis. And I think that your friend would not find confinement in our jail comfortable. Not even for a short stay."

I got up and went straight to the door before I could say something that would really get me in the soup. Bastard! Of course, he was bluffing. A respectable member of the international community was not going to be locked up on a bogus charge. I repeated that to myself several times with steadily diminishing conviction, concluding, at worse, that David might have to take a little trip to Spain. Return to England. Lay off the whiskey. We'd work something out.

I found him in the Petit Socco, alone and looking pensive. When he saw me, his face lit up, and he greeted me the way he had in the old days when we were just starting out together and everything was exciting. "A sight for sore eyes!" he cried and patted the seat next to him. "I'm so bored in Tangier. Let's take a trip."

"Good idea."

Before I could elaborate on the benefits of putting water between us and the commissioner, David said, "I've hired a car and organized a picnic. We're off down the coast, mountains and the Med. What are we staying in this sewer for? Tell me that!"

"No reason," I said.

At the gate of the medina we met a driver with an elegant, if elderly, Peugeot and set off. About an hour down the coast, we stopped on a scrubby green slope that overlooked a tiny white beach amid weathered rock formations like abstract sculptures.

David loved the sun, the water, the sand, and at that precise moment, stepping out on the tarmac with the empty sea and empty beach and empty hills, he seemed happier than he had been for a long time. Though I'm an urban man, myself, and always keen to put a good layer of concrete between myself and nature, I scrambled eagerly down to the water after him, while our driver found a shady spot and lit up a pipe filled with kef.

We had a picnic. David swam in the azure water while I splashed in the shallows. When he said with a wicked gleam in his eye, "I think you've been a bad boy," I agreed enthusiastically. Leaving aside the sand, sex al fresco can suit me fine.

We were lying on the blanket, watching the sky begin to turn pink. "I never should have left the country," he remarked. "Quiet is good for me."

I was struck by this; David rarely talked about his precarious state of mind and his gaudy troubles. "Well, go back," I said. "You have your house in Berks. And what about the cottage in Bermuda. That's near a beach, isn't it?"

"All gone. I've rather run through my resources, Francis. I'm having a hard time making the rent here. Drink and boys will empty one's pockets."

That was a shock. David had been independently wealthy when I first met him. "But you have skills."

He held out his hands. They were trembling, despite two bottles of wine at lunch and surreptitious shots of whiskey on the way. "I can't fly now."

"There's your music. You're very gifted."

"Yes, I must become a piano man. Fancy parties a possibility, do you think?"

"I should think so! You'll charm all the old queens and the dowagers, too." But even as I spoke, I wondered. There had been too many incidents, quarrels, sudden explosions of irrational wrath.

"We'll see, but I rather think some seedy cafe. More reliable liquor." There was a bitter tone to his words. Alcohol made me merry, but it made him sad. Yet without it, he was prey to horrors and regrets and terrors. The commissioner was right. David would not survive in a Moroccan prison, and leaving was no longer an option for him. I knew that he'd need to be careful, but for a time, all the omens were good. We went for rides in the afternoon and explored the rugged terrain to the east of the city and even skirted the desert with its bare ground the very color of the unprimed canvases I favor. No more astute than other mortals, I allowed myself to hope that David's demons slept and that the commissioner would find someone else knowledgeable to assist his investigation.

Then came a night at the Meridian, when David's face grew dark as he nursed his whiskey. A young German was next to us at the bar, and maybe it was no more than the echo of certain guttural vowels, but David began muttering to himself and without warning picked up the barman's cocktail fork and stabbed the boy in the arm. The evening deteriorated from there.

Early the next morning, I collected David at the police station. There was bail to be paid and apologies and not-so-veiled threats. David was shaky and white, his whole demeanor gentle and sad. Even the gendarmes found his earlier rage almost inconceivable.

I put him, nearly weeping with shame, in a cab and walked down to the commissioner's HQ. When I was shown in, he handed me a business card, and I took it without a word and nodded. I was going to see a man about some pictures.

CHAPTER THREE

The gallery was just off the Avenue Pasteur, in a Spanish Colonial building with small, high windows protected by iron grills and equipped with a wooden door fit to withstand a siege. A shiny brass plate in a handsome script read: GOLDFARBER GALLERY, PAINTINGS AND OBJETS D'ART FOR THE DISCERNING. I pushed the matching brass bell and waited.

When the door opened, I got a surprise. Herr Goldfarber was not at all what I'd expected, being a massive and robust man with blond hair and a boxer's nose. If I'd seen him on the street in Soho, I'd have taken him for one of Billy Hill's gangsters.

"*Guten tag*," I said. It had been a long time since I'd used my German, picked up, like so much of my education, on the fly and on the street.

"*Ah, Sie sprechen Deutsch! Welkommen, welkommen.*"

I was ushered in. A small foyer opened to a handsome exhibition space with a handful of nicely hung and well-framed paintings. I introduced myself. There was no point in deception because the foreign colony was small enough so that any import was instant news. My name, reputation, and connections would have been all around the Mountain within hours of my arrival at the port.

Herr Goldfarber professed delight in meeting me, especially in exchanging remarks in his native tongue. "And such a good accent. Berlin, I believe?"

I nodded.

"One could wish elsewhere, but still an excellent accent. It takes me back." He beamed, the very image of the sophisticated dealer, then cracked his knuckles, which rather spoiled the effect. He was like an elephant serving tea, remarkable in itself but somehow unconvincing.

"I saw the Picasso you sold Richard Alleyn," I said. "I just had to come and admire."

"Of course! Nothing quite that fine at the moment, I'm afraid, but I have a nice little Matisse drawing and this," he gestured toward a fine Derain landscape.

It was good, I could see that, and I'd have bet that the Matisse drawing, at least, was authentic. "Unfortunately, my wallet doesn't stretch quite that far. In fact, although I was here on holiday, I'm afraid I'll have to get back to the easel. Does anyone in Tangier deal in artist supplies?"

Thanks to my Moroccan student, whom I'd gifted with some used canvases, I knew there was not. Goldfarber shook his head regretfully. "Painting has not flourished here. The Muslim prohibition against images had left us only their splendid tile work."

I wandered around the room. At least two more works, a Picasso still life and a semiabstract Stuart Davis were clearly bogus. I guessed a Picasso ink drawing and another Matisse charcoal were not. What exactly was Goldfarber's game? I turned from my examination of a nice little Braque, a copy extraordinaire in my opinion, to find him watching me with a speculative air. *Oh, ho, Francis.* I could see that things might develop in an interesting way with a little assistance such as I know how to provide. I learned a lot more than German verbs in wicked old Berlin.

"Have you any more drawings?" I asked. "The Matisses and the Picasso are very fine."

"I see that you're a connoisseur. Most of my clients like the bright and colorful. Drawings, now, are the real artist's love. Yes?"

"Without a doubt," I said.

"I keep some in the back. In my personal quarters."

Emphasis on personal; he gave my *hind* quarters a glance, too. We now had a kittenish elephant. Was assisting the toad-like commissioner worth my virtue? Since *Mein Herr* was just my type, I thought I could make the sacrifice. I said I'd love to see his drawings—and anything else on offer—and followed him into a combined store room, office, and bedroom—where, for the next hour, we combined business and pleasure.

Later, out in the sharp, late afternoon light, I counted my visit a success. I found a phone in the souk and called the commissioner. "I can tell you this," I said. "Whatever Herr Goldfarber is, he's not a Jew."

"Really?"

"On the best possible eye-witness evidence."

"That calls into question his documents. We've made an excellent start."

I didn't think *he* had made anything except difficulties for me. "I feel I've earned that arrest warrant."

"All in good time, Monsieur Francis, all in good time. We need a little more before we can question a respectable member of the Zone."

I was annoyed rather than disappointed, having anticipated

that I would not escape so easily. "More might be possible. I'm to see him tomorrow. He hinted that he might have some work for me." Indeed, he had done more than hint. I had the promise, at least, of two hundred pounds sterling.

"Very good, Monsieur Francis. I see I was not mistaken in your talents. Report to me every day, but be careful."

"Top of my agenda," I said and hung up.

The next afternoon I returned to the blond elephant. We adjourned to the back room where all was quite exciting—a big dash of the sinister is very much in my line. Just the same, I could tell that Goldfarber was nervous. Afterward, he made himself a pipe of kef, toxic stuff in my experience, and lay on his divan, smoking. The drug didn't seem to produce much effect, but perhaps it enabled him to reach a decision, because he said, "I have a problem, Francis. A delicate problem."

I waited.

"I promised a painting that I cannot deliver."

"I've had that experience," I said, thinking most unwillingly of recent exaggerations, if not outright lies, to my gallery about work done and quality produced. "My dealer, however, is a gem and sympathetic."

"Would I were in your shoes, Francis." And he sighed.

"Is the painting lost?"

"Unfinished. It needs extensive restoration."

"Ah." Here was the opening the commissioner desired for me, where, instead of poverty and indifference, the unlucky painter risked having his throat cut. Then I thought of David. I had posted bail for him, but that could be revoked. I knew it could. "I could possibly help you out," I said. "I have a certain skill."

He reached over the pillow and put one massive hand around my throat. And squeezed. "It's a delicate matter requiring the utmost discretion," he said.

I nodded and began to gasp. He took his hand away, but it was several minutes before I could breathe normally. "Asthma," I said.

"So much the better." At moments, Goldfarber's eyes strongly reminded me of the commissioner's; they were quarried from the same stone. Then he patted my shoulder. "Nothing personal," he said. "Outside of business, I really like you very much."

Goldfarber locked up his establishment, and we drove south down the avenue. It was a dull, damp day with a light wind off the water that stirred, rather than dispersed, the thick odors of bad drains and raw sewage. Despite the desert at its back, the city had all the usual drawbacks of seaside towns except nosy landladies.

Goldfarber took a variety of small streets, then circled back toward the center. The realization that he was making sure no one was on our tail did nothing to reassure me. Finally, he stopped at an ugly, anonymous building, one of the cheap modern constructions lacking both the solid comforts of the Mountain and the dodgy charms of the medina. There was a cafe on the lower floor where Arab men wearing red fezzes and Western slacks smoked kef and drank mint tea. A wide green awning provided a shady patch for a gaggle of half-naked shoeshine boys. Goldfarber stomped through their midst, muttering under his breath and giving them baleful looks.

"I hate Arabs," he remarked as we took the stairs. "Filthy beggars. Steal you blind."

That explained a lot. Here he was in the paradise of pretty boys, and he was reduced to making eyes at Yours Truly. And what about the dead Spaniard? More business and pleasure? *Keep alert, Francis!*

The upper floor was a sizable studio with a worktable and big padlocked cupboards, wide enough, I guessed, to store good-sized paintings. A professional easel held a canvas with what looked to be an outline drawing of a Picasso, a swooning image of his mistress Marie-Thérèse Walter, looking boneless and gentle. Not my favorite period and not, except for his etchings of her, my favorite subject, either. A rather faded color photo of the same image had been pinned up on the easel frame, and a few colors had been experimentally spotted around the canvas. If this was "restoration," I was the police commissioner of Tangier.

Goldfarber gave me a look. "Extensive work required, of course."

This was too ridiculous for comment. We were set to forge a large and valuable painting. "When is it expected?" I asked.

"End of the week."

I shook my head. "The oil paint will never be dry, not even if the wind shifts."

"It's due at the end of the week," he repeated. "And, of course, since it was painted in the thirties, it will be dry."

I couldn't help noticing his fingers twitching. "Right," I said. "Paint as dry as possible. Tempera underneath maybe? Have you any? It dries fast and takes oil over it. The technique of the old masters."

He'd already laid out some good quality European-made oil paints, lovely but slow to dry. I rather hoped he didn't have tempera, because the only water-based paint I've used was gouache, the designer's medium. Luck was not with me; Goldfarber quickly found some jars of dry pigment.

I could foresee a tricky preparation with egg yolks, and besides, glaze on top of tempera was hardly typical of Picasso. I again checked the color photo. "Another thought. Can you buy house paint in the city? Emulsion dries in a day or two. We could certainly use that for the background and in place of the 'fat,' slower-drying colors."

Goldfarber thought for a moment then put his heavy hand on my shoulder. "Make a list," he said.

When I'd written down the most useful colors, he told me to start work and went out, locking the door behind him. That was how I began my stint as an art forger. Not so physically demanding as the interior decoration I've been forced to do in my career, nor so awkward as a little spell as a seaside portraitist, but in some ways less congenial than either. I don't lie in painting, though I lie easily in life. "It's for a good cause, Francis," I told myself, but I wasn't sure I believed that. Everything about the business was murky except for David's troubles and the dead Spanish boy.

A dead painter was close to home, anyway, and I sat down to study the drawing and think about appropriate colors. When Goldfarber returned with a carton holding assorted cans of house paint and some mixing buckets, I set to work approximating the master's soft candy colors and rich, deep purples.

Bit of a challenge, really, but the paint was quite good quality, and it went on fast and smooth. When I was first learning to paint—on the fly again from a lover who is now old and terribly respectable—I worked just like this. Lay out a drawing of mostly geometric shapes with black paint, then fill in the shapes with colors.

I worked until I began to lose the light. "I can't do any more today," I said.

Goldfarber roused himself from where he'd been smoking and came over to check my work.

"It's complete!" he exclaimed. "This is good."

"Not quite." I pointed out some little missing details. "I don't dare attempt the features in this light. It would be way too easy to make mistakes. And it's best to let everything dry overnight."

His hostile and speculative look gave me a new and clear understanding of the old story of Scheherazade.

"It's almost done," he said impatiently. "Put in her face and fingernails, and get finished."

"If you want it ruined, I'll go ahead. But the paint is still wet underneath and wet into wet won't have the right effect. Besides, I'll never match the colors now." The foggy gray light that filled the narrow windows was sinking into thick shadows all around the room. The studio had a gasoline lamp to supplement the unreliable electricity, but neither it nor the two lonely ceiling bulbs was adequate. "Impossible."

"First thing tomorrow," he said. "First thing!"

"I paint in the mornings," I said, momentarily forgetting I'd claimed to be out of supplies. "I'll see you in the afternoon. When we have a chance that this will be dry."

I thought he was going to go for my throat again, but instead he laid a heavy hand on my shoulder. "Touch up then," he said.

"And off to your client at the weekend." I smiled to encourage him, and perhaps the kef had taken effect, for he seemed to relax. Just the same, I was uneasy having him at my back down the steep stairs, and I was relieved when he drove away. I hoofed it back toward the medina with thoughts of a cafe, of meeting David, of passing an amusing evening. I had not gone very far when the dull day gave way to the quick nightfall of the Mediterranean, and the fog turned to a gusty rain.

Perhaps that is why I did not notice the man until I was slipping on the greasy, garbage-strewn stones of a narrow alley, and trying to use the awnings of the little shops to avoid the downpour. I was beginning to see the attractions of hooded Moroccan garments when I noticed a man examining a display of pots despite the streaming rain. He was tall and thin, and when he gave me a quick, surreptitious glance, I saw that he was blond—one of the international community.

That was a bad sign. Despite rivalry and dislike amounting to hatred among the various ethnic and religious rivals in the city, serious violence from the locals was quite rare. I doubted now that a Moroccan had killed the Spanish boy—or, indeed, that the commissioner would have press-ganged me if he had not suspected a foreigner.

I left the shelter of the awning and hurried to the next corner. I wanted to get to one of the larger streets, where I hoped that, despite the rain, there would be enough shoppers and vendors for me to elude my pursuer. When a woman with a huge umbrella and a large basket momentarily blocked the alley behind me, I squeezed between a tiny storefront and a still warm brazier to a covered passage with steps down to a wider lane below. The steep descent stank of urine and drains and the salty dampness of the coast had coated the walls with greenish slime.

I clattered down, frightening a pair of skinny cats, and recognized where I was. Three buildings to the left, I pounded urgently on a blue-painted door.

"*Prego,*" someone called. The door opened, and I nipped inside a dimly lit space with the smell of kef, perfume, and sweat. The brothel keeper was an Italian of Falstaffian proportions, swathed in a crimson velvet smoking robe like an Edwardian gentleman. His impressive head with its aquiline nose, fine black mustache, and blue shadowed cheeks was topped with an amazing, if ill-advised, blond wig. His establishment was considered reputable for its type, and his stable of boys was both large and eclectic.

I scrambled in my wallet for some bills. "A treat for a friend, who will be along momentarily," I said, pressing the money into his damp white hand.

"*Grazie,*" he said, and he inclined his head in a courtly manner.

"Now I need to leave by the rear door. Immediately."

The vagaries of his profession had given the proprietor a sangfroid that was not easily disturbed. "Of course, *signor*. This way."

He escorted me through a carved fretwork door into a candle-lit salon full of lounging boys with kohl-rimmed eyes and painted children old beyond their years. They were draped in blankets against the chill, and before they could reveal their naked glory, we were in the corridor to the private rooms and the kitchen. A wave to the tall black cook at the stove, a hasty thanks to the proprietor, and I was out the door. I hoped that my pursuer would take advantage of my generosity. But even if he proved immune to the charms of the establishment, there would be momentary confusion and, at the very least, no access to the rear exit.

I ran until my asthma played up, then, soaking wet and shivering, I found a cab and made my way to one of the better hotels. The food was only fair, but the electricity was on, the sight lines in the restaurant were excellent, and there was a quite private phone off the bar.

"The painting is nearly done," I told the commissioner. "Final details tomorrow and probably varnishing the next day if this filthy weather clears."

"Excellent."

"That's the good news," I said. "But I was followed through the medina. And Goldfarber is nervous."

I detailed the dealer's evasive route to the studio and described the man who'd followed me as well as I could.

"Where are you to meet Goldfarber tomorrow?" the commissioner asked. He seemed untroubled by my narrow escape.

"At the studio," I said, "but I'd rather not go. As soon as the paint is dry, he may figure he can do the finishing himself. Besides, you can arrest him at any time."

"We want his customer," the commissioner said. "And have you been paid? No? He will be suspicious if you don't show up."

"Meanwhile, I risk having my throat cut like that poor Spaniard."

"We are not sure Goldfarber is the killer," the commissioner said smoothly. "We've had him under surveillance, and his alibi is good. Do not worry about him, Monsieur Francis." And he hung up before I could ask who I should worry about. It's a sad fact of the artist's life that one is often considered expendable.

I gave the bartender some more coins and called David.

"Where have you been?" His voice was querulous.

"Hither and yon," I said. "Come to the Palace. We'll have dinner. And bring me a sweater. I got soaked in the rain."

"Serves you right," he said. "You put me in a cab and disappeared when I was too sick to walk straight."

"I bailed you out, too, if you remember. That produced complications that I've been dealing with. Bring me a sweater," I repeated and hung up. I was wet, cold, and angry, and though I adored David, he was an ungrateful bastard. I ordered a coffee with cognac and sat at a table toward the back, shivering in the damp, nursing resentment, and trying to decide if I would return to Goldfarber's studio. I was under no obligation, none at all. He could finish the final details and varnish the painting himself.

After all, forgery! Of all the things I detest, painting in someone else's style for profit is high on the list. And the worst of it was the picture wasn't half-bad. Let it dry, put in the last touches, have it gather dust for a while. Add a few nicks in the surface, some dirt on the stretcher, and the effort of one afternoon would pass muster in half the galleries of Europe. It struck me that Tangier was capable of fashioning a temptation to fit every soul.

The lights flickered overhead, and the barman prudently lit several candelabras, adding the smell of melting wax to the spices of the restaurant and the omnipresent breath of the drains. I thought it might be good for me to leave the city for a time. And take David. A trip to the Spanish Zone, maybe, or to Marrakech, though David's chance of crossing any of the borders would be nil at the moment.

But I could go, and I was thinking that I might, that even a little run out into the desert might be interesting, when the electricity blinked out. The candelabra on the bar became the sole bright spot, darkness hanging in sheets behind it like the striated backgrounds of my pope paintings. Life imitates art, and one's imaginings are realized in surprising ways, at unexpected times.

In a moment, the waiters were hustling around with candles for the tables. The restaurant, banal in modern lighting, took on an air of fantasy with dozens of little flickering lights that picked out the diners in golden light and umber shadows.

I was enjoying the effect when an unfamiliar British voice said my name from the darkness behind me. I turned. There was a man seated at the next table. I hadn't heard him come in with the bustle and complaints of the blackout.

"You are?"

"No need for introductions," he said. "Just remember we're watching you. You'd do well to be careful. Tangier isn't what it was."

"You're from the legation," I guessed. All the European powers, plus the Americans, had legations in Tangier. Their officials were fixtures in the restaurants and at all the best parties. I tried to see if this one was tall, thin, and blond like my pursuer this afternoon, but he had extinguished his candle, and he was just a slightly darker shape, flickering in the neighboring lights.

"That's of no matter. Just watch yourself, Mr. Bacon. Her Majesty's Government can only offer so much protection."

"You followed me today," I said, but with a rustle and the scrape of his chair, he was gone. I stood up, eager to confront him, but now a waiter approached, and I saw David, burdened with an umbrella and bearing a sweater and my leather jacket.

"You look marvelous by candlelight," he joked. He began to sing "Moonlight Becomes You," so that the restaurant patrons—who had been grousing as they were wont to do whenever the power went—began to laugh and clap, acknowledging the beauty of the moment. That was David's gift. The other side of drunken rages and needless cruelty was a knack for lending intensity to a moment, for bringing it out of the boring and ordinary and making it memorable.

He sat down in an expansive mood. "We'll have lamb, right? And couscous and one of the salads. And I'll have a double whiskey," he told the waiter. "Things will be marvelous again, won't they?" he asked me so I understood that he was trying hard, that he'd been all at sea or in the air or wherever it was he went, and now he was back on dry land and things would be all right.

With me, too. And then I felt annoyed. What the hell did Her Majesty's Government mean by spying on me? Sneaking up to whisper warnings and chasing me down the alleys of the medina. They could go to hell. At that moment, with David smiling across the table and looking, with the help of whiskey and candles, as he had that night long ago in the Gargoyle, I thought I'd send the commissioner and his schemes to the same address.

CHAPTER FOUR

Candles lend enchantment, but morning light is a different matter. Even a perfect blue-and-gold Mediterranean dawn has a way of casting the pall of reason over one's affairs. Even though David seemed cheerful again, our troubles were not over, because I was short of money. Short enough that I'd composed yet another heartfelt, if not exactly truthful, missive to my gallery. I hinted at marvelous things accomplished—or to be accomplished soon—and assurances of hard work and of good relations with the Muse.

Of all this, only the reference to hard work bore any relation to reality, for that very morning I had taken a knife to a disappointing *Pope* and consigned another *Owl* canvas to my Moroccan friend. Although I calculated to the penny how much my dealer would send me—and how soon the transfer might arrive—even the most optimistic math left me short. Two hundred pounds from Goldfarber was no trifle. After making a hash of my latest canvas, I was inclined to take the commissioner's assessment of the dealer at face value and return to finish that dodgy "Picasso."

But first, a visit to Richard was in order. He'd gotten me into the mess, and since he was connected to everyone of consequence, I figured that he'd know if the legation was involved. I cleaned my brushes and took a cab up the Mountain. The brilliant sea was dotted with little ships and gulls swooped overhead. At a certain elevation on sunny days, Tangier is a travel agent's dream.

Richard was in his garden, fussing with lemon trees and roses, lavenders and quinces. "Francis! What a lovely surprise! You've escaped the clutches of the law."

"Where you put me, Richard." I was not in the mood for his camp antics. Given the situation, he might at least let me have the amusing lines.

"Public duty, old man, public duty."

"Indeed," I said, "which I've discharged."

"Come in and tell me all." He shouted for his servant to bring us coffee and led me to the courtyard with a fountain burbling away and his parrot squawking from the fig tree.

"It was really too bad of the commissioner to send me home ignorant the other day. As though he didn't trust my discretion." He gave me a look of feigned indignation.

The commissioner was right about that. Gossip was Richard's stock-in-trade and a source of his power, but I just shrugged. "He spared you a boring interview. He wanted to talk about paintings."

"I didn't think the commissioner a connoisseur." In his own way, Richard was shrewd.

"Fakes, though, catch his interest."

"A shocking business. Really shocking. I was quite taken in."

I wondered about that. In retrospect, Richard had seemed less regretful of his purchase than eager to involve the police. Like almost everyone else in Tangier, he had complex agendas. "You hadn't dealt with this Goldfarber before?"

"I dealt with his predecessor, Peter Simon, a lovely man, lovely. He got a visa to the states and moved—a year or so ago. Relatives in Miami, I believe. Goldfarber took over the gallery then. He seemed respectable enough."

"Any idea where his stock came from?"

"The commissioner wanted to know that, too. But I have no idea. He had the usual dealer patter: family collection, broken up with hard times, plus purchases from his fellow refugees. Rather more of the latter than the former in his case."

I sensed that was correct. The next step was delicate, but I decided I had to take it. "You know, I stopped by the gallery the other day. Just out of curiosity."

"Oh, dear, I don't think anyone wants to patronize him now," Richard sniffed. Goldfarber had been banished, and cursed were all who trafficked with him. In the maintenance of polite society, Richard was as ruthless as Genghis Khan.

"I couldn't agree more; forgery is beyond the pale. But listen, Richard, here's the thing: I had a peek at Goldfarber's stock, and I'm certain that the drawings, at least, are authentic."

"Really!" Richard's eyes lit up with the prospect of acquisition. Then his face fell. "Still, it's impossible, old man. Quite impossible."

Naturally, I agreed, though I wouldn't have been surprised to see Richard's Mercedes parked outside the gallery one day soon. "Anyway, when I was walking back through the medina, I was followed."

Richard winked. "I should think that a fairly common occurrence. Some of us are still young and beautiful."

"It was pouring with rain. Simply bucketing down."

"Passion, my dear," he said in a reminiscent tone. "I remember it well."

"He was tall, thin—and blond."

Richard raised his eyebrows. "Mad dogs and Englishmen go out in the pouring rain, too, apparently," he said, but he didn't sound quite so amused.

"Right. My thought was British legation. And knowing that you know everyone in Tangier in every legation—"

"Tall, blond, and thin? Not an awful lot to go on, is there?" he asked rather sharply. It was surprising how quickly Richard dropped the camp act when his interest was engaged. And now I remembered something else about him: despite his fussy mannerisms and desperate respectability, he'd "had a good war," as they said. I'd not stopped to consider the implications of that. Everyone attributed his presence in Tangier to his sexual tastes and his family's eminence. I wondered now if that was just the half of it, and if he had other, more interesting reasons for residing in the Zone.

If he did, Richard was too cunning to reveal them to a security risk like me; painters haven't been judged reliable since the days of Rubens and Velasquez. But Richard's pose of ignorance, the absence of the usual legation gossip, and his easy dismissal of my interesting story were revealing. Possibly the legation had found me suspicious or, belatedly, Her Majesty's Government had taken an interest in my safety.

Either one suggested that there must be more to Goldfarber's business than defrauding gullible art lovers. Though people have died for art, I didn't think his particular forgeries were valuable enough to have led to murder. And there was another thing: Could I assume the commissioner was correct that the murdered Spanish boy had been "restoring" canvases for Goldfarber?

I had accepted his word rather naively, when all I'd seen was a black-and-white photo. Did I even know the corpse was Spanish and a painter? I decided I did not. I didn't entirely trust Richard, whom I knew and liked. I decided I should give even less credence to the commissioner, whom I didn't like and couldn't fathom.

On my way back to town, I considered the manifold possibilities for crime in Tangier. Smuggling and currency manipulation were the runaway favorites, employing folks rich and poor, but as far as I could see, Goldfarber wasn't trying to smuggle pictures. He was selling them openly and had probably done all right until he sold that bone period Picasso. Richard had either developed doubts about it or—and this was more serious from my point of view—had spotted the fake right away and decided to use it to curry favor with the new commissioner.

Both scenarios were possible, but could Richard have another agenda? I thought that I'd like to learn more about the murder of the Spanish boy, which had been kept oddly quiet. Murders in the International Zone were rare, murders of the foreign population almost unheard of. Yet had there been anything in the press?

My dear Nan would have been able to tell me, being a great fan of crime news, which she'd followed avidly via the dailies. I'd pretty much given weird killings and sensational passions a miss since her death, but newspapers keep archives, and I could check the French dailies, *Le Petite Moroccan* and *Le Journal de Tangier*, as well as the weekly English-language *Tangier Gazette and Moroccan Mail*.

Securing the newspaper files would doubtless require a good many drinks with local pressmen, and to fund these inquiries, I needed money. I decided to keep my appointment with Goldfarber, but at two p.m., when I climbed the stairs to the studio, I found the door locked. It seemed I was early, although he'd been very insistent on my getting the picture done as soon as possible. I decided to wait in the cafe below.

I was seated and sipping the mint concoction of the city, when I noticed how quiet the cafe was. Not silent, you understand, for the radio was blaring the usual high North African voices, swooping and howling over flutes, strings, and drums. I'm not a fan of music in general and of the local ditties in particular. There was the noise from the street—cars and carts and vendors shouting outside, too. Although the cafe was almost full, the rooms, or rather the patrons, were quiet.

They'd been talking and noisy when I passed on my way to the stairs. Now conversation had dropped, if not stopped altogether, and I was aware of being studied. The crowd was young, the proper age for the new revolutionaries and fanatics, political and religious, and there was not another European in the room. For the first time in Tangier, I felt uncomfortable.

Although there was nothing to distinguish this cafe from dozens of others, I was definitely unwelcome, even though one expected a mixed Arab and European clientele in the newer town. Richard might be right after all: change was in the air, and it was sweeping from the medina toward the European town and the Mountain. I finished the tea, paid the waiter, and left as the sound of excited voices rose behind me.

The cafe was a strange one, and it was particularly odd that Goldfarber, supposedly a Jew, had picked that building for his studio. Surely he would have been alert to the unfriendly clientele. Then I reminded myself that Goldfarber was not Jewish at all and that he might have reasons for renting above that very cafe. What those reasons might be, I hadn't the faintest idea.

I walked idly for a bit, admired some rugs, and contemplated the purchase of a burnoose made of coarse white wool, a practical garment now that the weather was getting colder. The vendor and I haggled over the price, and after the requisite quarter of an hour, I walked away with the cloak over my arm. When a chilly wind blew up off the water, I slipped the burnoose over my head and caught a glimpse of my reflection in one of the shop windows. What a change in silhouette! Though my sun-bleached hair gave me away, at a quick glance I looked quite different, and before I passed back in front of the cafe, I pulled the hood up over my head and hustled up the stairs.

The door was still locked. I gave it a thump and a kick for good measure but got no response. With possibilities multiplying like rats, I hurried to the main avenue and hailed a cab. "Goldfarber Gallery off Avenue Pasteur," I told the driver. Maybe Goldfarber had changed his mind about the painting, but I hadn't changed mine about that two hundred pounds.

Indeed, my mind was so firmly on my finances that I forgot to take off the burnoose and ignored the blustery wind that blew the hood up over my hair. At the gallery, I pushed the bell and waited, then tried again. When there was no response, I leaned on the button and let the bell keep ringing. In time, I heard the crisp sound of the bolt being drawn, followed by the rattle of the latch.

The door swung open, and I was inside before he recognized me.

When he did, he wasn't pleased. "Francis! What the hell are you doing?" Goldfarber's heavy face was flushed and angry. "Why are you here?"

"A better question is why weren't you at the studio? We were supposed to meet more than an hour ago."

"Something came up." Goldfarber was not just irritated but nervous. He jerked the door open and said, "I can't deal with you now. Get out and come back later."

"You owe me two hundred pounds," I said. "Pay me and I'm off in a moment."

"You'll leave now if you know what's good for you." He shoved the door shut again, suggesting that he didn't want anyone to see me.

"You have your painting. I want my money." I counted on his nervous eagerness to give me what I wanted, and although he was tempted to threaten and perhaps to attack, he thrust his hand into his pocket and pulled out a bundle of cash.

"Now get out of here," he said.

Before I could put the money into my wallet, Goldfarber had opened the door and laid one of his large hands on the back of my neck. I expected to be launched onto the sidewalk, but suddenly I was propelled back into the gallery with a burst of German profanity that really did take me aback.

He slid the bolt in the door and turned to me with a wild look. "You must not be seen here!"

"Is there a rear exit?"

Instead of answering, he grabbed my arm and rushed me across the gallery to a dark and narrow corridor with stairs along one side. At the end was a tall, old-fashioned door. He unlocked it, but instead of stepping outside, I was shoved inside a glorified closet. I shouted and threw my weight against the door, but he'd already turned the key. Then the bell rang, high and insistent, drowning out my complaints. With another burst of distinctly low German, Goldfarber ran to the front of the building.

I figured this was the important visitor, the one he'd opened the door for only to find yours truly. It was interesting that I'd been wearing the local garb at the time, suggesting he'd expected a Moroccan. I put my ear to the door. Across the gallery came the murmur of voices. I thought that I could distinguish Goldfarber's, but the substance, even the language, of their conversation was impossible to determine. They crossed the tiled gallery, and I shrank away from the door against the wall. Goldfarber was a formidable specimen; I was not keen to meet someone who could put the wind up him.

I waited for their approach, but the footsteps faded again. Another little session in the back room? If so, discretion was the order of the day; I heard nothing. I might have been alone in the building. Had they managed to leave unheard? I was beginning to wheeze from nerves and dust, and my legs had started to prickle and fall asleep, when I thought I heard steps in the gallery again.

I put my ear to the door. Stealthy footsteps? I thought so. And another ambiguous swishing sound. Was something being dragged across the floor? That was a bad sound, bringing with it a bad thought. Now the door. Visitor leaving? I waited. To call while the mysterious guest was on the premises might be disastrous. But what if Goldfarber left with his visitor? The building had thick walls; the little store room had a stout door. I could be there for quite a while.

I'm not fond of dark, enclosed places at the best of times, and I didn't fancy being left in a commercial building that might be closed for days. Maybe longer, depending on just what had transpired between Goldfarber and his visitor. Soon my anxiety about what might happen when the dealer returned was replaced by the fear that he might not return at all.

By this time, my eyes had adjusted to the darkness, broken only by a strip of light seeping in over the threshold. The door, afflicted with wood worm or dry rot, was shy of the floor. Just how long had I been inside? I lay down, an awkward business, as there seemed to be storage racks protruding from every side and stuck my watch close to the little band of light: four p.m. It felt much later, but still I'd been there over an hour. Whether Goldfarber was coming back or not, I wanted to get out.

Think, Francis. That's what my old Nan used to say whenever I was in a pickle. I leaned against the door, rattled the handle, and peered into the keyhole. That was blocked by the key. I got off the floor and began to explore the racks. Framed pictures, canvases, and then a stack of—what? Portfolios. Yes, with paper, drawings, and prints. I took one out. Nice heavy paper, thick and strong. I slid it under the door and positioned it beneath the lock.

In Nan's detective stories, people were always equipped with knitting needles or locksmith's picks or pocketknives with useful blades. I returned to the storage racks. Most of the canvases were still unframed, but at least one of the smaller framed pictures had its hanging wire, which I unwound from the eye hooks. Stiff enough? *You won't know until you try, Francis.*

I began a delicate operation with the wire, trying not to let the frayed ends get stuck but still using enough force to dislodge the key. After several abortive tries, I doubled up the wire and gave a good sharp push. The key rattled out of the lock. I took a deep breath before I peeked under the door. Had I pushed too hard? Had the key bounced off the paper? I squashed my face against the floor and squinted. No key. Not that I could see.

By this time, my breathing had been reduced to a rasping wheeze. I seized the edge of the paper, and, so as not to tip the key off if it should be there, I slid the drawing carefully back under the door. Steady, steady. A little *clink*—that was the key hitting the bottom of the door. Now to get it under. I tried to keep my lungs operational until I got the tips of two fingers on the key.

I struggled to slide it inside despite the uneven lower edge of the door. I made several attempts and used most of my vocabulary before I maneuvered the key close to the door jamb and flicked it inside. I stood up, gasping, to try the lock. The mechanism was old and loose, but after several minutes I persuaded the wards to engage and the door to open.

I looked down at the floor. Light from the narrow gallery windows revealed that I'd made use of a Balthus drawing. I felt better;

he's not one of my favorites. Just the same, I returned it carefully to the portfolio. Like him or not, he's a fine draftsman.

I was locking up the store room when I heard a noise at the front door. Goldfarber returning? I left the key in the lock and bolted for the stairs. I managed two steps before the door opened. I pressed against the wall of the stairwell and tried not to breathe.

"Hello," someone called. "Is the gallery open?" There was something familiar about the voice, but I thought it best to stay where I was. "Herr Goldfarber?"

"Something fishy here," said another voice.

"Have a quick look around, shall we?"

The voice sounded like Richard's. Could he have come to see the drawings and buy one on the sly? I was about to call out to him, when I heard him say, "Look for any records, financial documents. We may not get such a good chance again."

I shut my mouth and started backing cautiously up the stairs. I had almost reached the top when I heard steps in the corridor. I froze again. Whoever it was had only to look up. Even in the dim light I'd be visible, and now I regretted not calling out to them.

There was a shout from below. "Something's not right here; come look at this."

Richard—I definitely recognized his voice even without the little camp jokes and unctuous gentility—said, "Be right there," and he walked back to the gallery.

There were three doors at the top of the stairs. One was locked. One was a bathroom, and one led to the roof. Roofs are all right. Fire watching with Arnold during the war got me over any fear of heights. I hurried up the iron stairs and came out into the late sunlight. I was looking over an expanse of roofs, some with pigeon houses and potted figs, some with awnings over chairs and tables. Fortunately, no women in sight as yet. The Muslim ladies of

Morocco keep to the home. Their outings are to the roof gardens in the evening, and it's the worst of bad form for foreign men to be on roofs overlooking theirs. As I was now. I needed a ladder. An outside staircase. The wings of the Muse.

Richard and his friend were searching the gallery. I was pretty sure of that. Would they come upstairs? Yes, I thought they would. Would they bother with the roof? Uncertain. There was what I took to be a water tank and a little shed that held a generator for emergency power. That was interesting, but perhaps Goldfarber really did live in the gallery, and that convenient divan was not just for fun and games.

On my circuit around the roof, I noticed a rickety ladder against the water tank. Though hampered by the burnoose, I scrambled up. Ah, a covered top with a shallow slope. I tested it cautiously. I didn't fancy being drowned like the Duke of Clarence. Shakespeare gave him some decent wine for his fatal tumble; I'd probably get dodgy water and mosquito larvae.

But Richard and his friend would certainly come up if I weren't hidden. One of the laws of the universe is that when I'm in a pickle, things can only get worse. I stepped over the edge and very cautiously tested the top of the tank. A creak, a little groaning protest from wood and old metal but nothing more. I lay as flat as I could and waited.

The evening wind stirred up, brisk and cold. I checked my watch for what seemed the fiftieth time. If I waited too long, they would be gone, but Goldfarber might be back. I'd decided to risk descending, and I actually had one foot over the edge when I heard steps. Back onto the top with creaking and groaning. *No sudden moves, Francis!*

"It's got to be here somewhere," Richard said.

"Damned if I see where. We may be wrong, you know. He may

use somewhere else." That was the friend. I lifted my head cautiously. He was young, quite a bit younger than Richard, and blond. Thin, too. Well, well, my admirer from the medina. So much for youth and beauty and the passions of strangers.

"Maybe, but I think not," Richard said.

I dropped my head and listened to them moving around on the roof. The door of the shed opened. No joy there, apparently, because they resumed walking back and forth. Then I heard Richard laugh. "Well, would you look at that."

Had I been spotted? My lungs seized up, and I had a bad moment when I thought I must cough. The blond man began swearing.

"No one ever said Goldfarber was stupid," Richard said. He patted the water tank like a horse. "Wound his antenna around the tank. Hooked it up, my boy, when he made a transmission. I think we've rumbled him."

"Still, no sign of a transmitter."

"Oh, he'll keep that hidden. He knows we're onto it."

Footsteps now toward the stairs. A moment later, they were gone, and I sat up. The sky was rapidly darkening, and I saw few signs of electricity in the town below. Another outage. We might be dark for a few minutes or several hours. I needed to make my way back down before the building went totally black. I waited at the top of the outside stairs and listened. No sounds. I paused again at the top of the inner staircase, but the building remained silent. I crept down in complete darkness, flailed around for a moment, then felt my way along the corridor until I saw the faint rectangles of the gallery windows.

I felt my way along the wall toward the main door, and I was doing fine until a stout piece of ironwork caught me just above the ankle and pitched me onto the tiles with a great clatter and rattle. I clutched my leg, relieved my feelings with profanity in several languages, then groped in the blackness until I touched wrought iron. I'd tripped over one of the gallery's handsome standing candelabras, a useful decoration in a city with erratic power.

I got to my feet, set up the candelabra, and fumbled in my pocket for the matches that everyone, smoker or not, carried for just such emergencies. Once equipped with a candle, I decided to take a quick look in Goldfarber's inner sanctum. I found a few papers on the floor, a tipped over chair, but no real disarray. I suspected that Richard and his companion had tried to leave everything as they'd found it. Which meant that something had happened before Goldfarber left.

Something trivial, I thought, for there was no damage nor any sign of a serious struggle. In fact, as accustomed as I am to having spatters of paint everywhere, I almost missed the red spots on the edge of the desk. They were still sticky, and they looked like blood. Had Richard and his pal noticed them? Maybe, maybe not. They'd been after antennas and financial records, but, combined with that odd swishing sound and the single footsteps in the gallery, those little spots were a sign that either Goldfarber or his visitor had come to grief. *Get out of here, Francis!*

I was at the door before I thought of the faux Picasso. It tied me to Goldfarber, and if Richard should discover it, I'd be open to blackmail. Although I'm quite indifferent to the usual threats of sexual exposure, no serious painter can afford to be linked to forgery. I could almost hear Richard's usual campy speech sliding into the chilly and efficient voice I'd heard in the gallery. I could guess his price, too. Nothing so vulgar as money or even a painting. Rather, I'd be doing work for Tangier's new police commissioner, or perhaps for whatever mysterious British spy shop that employed Richard.

Neither was a good prospect, so though I was loath to do anything but make an immediate exit, I checked both the store room and the gallery. Nothing. Probably the faux Picasso was still locked up in the studio. I was stymied until I remembered Goldfarber opening the desk for the key. Watching at every step for any little drop of blood, I used my handkerchief to open the center drawer. Among a variety of keys, I recognized the square, modern Yale to the studio.

I hailed a cab well down the avenue and got out on the street behind the studio. Once upstairs, I hesitated, strongly tempted to leave both the "Picasso" and Goldfarber's dangerous orbit. But I had his key, probably the only one, and Richard and his pal either didn't know about the place or weren't interested in anything but transmitters. I unlocked the door and stepped inside. Naturally, my eye went first to the easel with a featureless Marie-Thérèse Walter in the middle of erotic reverie. She was nicely dry, too; I'd guessed right with the house paints.

I should, of course, have grabbed it and made my exit. But I couldn't resist putting in the last few lines of her closed eyes, soft mouth, and fingernails. I picked up a small, clean brush and opened a tin of black paint. One line, two, three: there was her face. Four, five, six: hands complete, and I'm not sure the master could have drawn them any better. I wiped the brush and, like a tidy artisan, went toward the sink where Goldfarber kept a container of turpentine.

It was only then that I noticed several crates piled near the sink with stacks of paint cans and a heap of canvas drop cloths. One cloth looked odd in a way I didn't much like. I moved closer and took a deep breath, then used the handle of the brush to lift one edge of the canvas. I saw the hair first, dark and matted with blood, then a tanned face with light expressionless eyes above a wide, broken nose and a toothy mouth with a trickle of blood at one corner. Not Moroccan, though he was wearing a burnoose. And not Goldfarber, either. This was a smaller, slighter man, identity unknown but status definite: the mysterious shock had happened. What was once alive, talking, scheming, fighting, playing was now so much raw meat.

The transformation had been recent, very recent by the look of him, and his skin was cool not cold. I was sure that this was the visitor whom Goldfarber had been nervously awaiting. Whatever his anxieties, they hadn't kept him from murder, and my heart started to hammer as I realized the narrowness of my escape, which I must now make good.

I was at the door before I glanced back at the easel. *Leave no evidence, Francis!* I took off the burnoose, wrapped the picture in it, and hustled downstairs.

CHAPTER FIVE

Fortunately the city's erratic electricity returned, or I would have walked right into the big Mercedes parked in front of my building. If I was not mistaken, the elegant white car belonged to Richard, last seen with a secret service–type combing through the Goldfarber Gallery. Not someone I wanted to meet at that moment, not with images of the dead man fresh in my mind and a forged Picasso tucked under my arm.

Quick turn to the left, head toward the water, take the hill to David's rented house. I saw lights upstairs and heard the sound of a jazz trumpet over a throbbing bass and a stride piano—the favorite record of a certain pretty beach boy. This was an evening for visits and entertaining, and I felt the thin, cold thread of jealousy. Irrational, really, when I am so fond of carrying on myself and of getting up to one thing or another, legal and otherwise. But love isn't rational.

The Greeks were right: irrationality leads to tears and violence and messes of one sort or another, such as those I am fond of depicting. Consider poor Phaedra, if you doubt me, or look at *The Bacchae*. Of course, in *The Bacchae*, neither rationality nor madness leads to salvation, which is more or less my view of life. The old dramatic poets of the Peloponnesus grasped the reality of the universe. I try for something similar, but when I get close to it on canvas, half the critics and most of the public are horrified that the results are so "violent," so "exaggerated."

They wouldn't know what I felt in David's front room, listening to the sounds floating down from above. My heart turned to fire, my head to ice, and my skin shriveled away and sloughed off, leaving my nerves bare. That's what I strive to put on canvas, and it doesn't look very polite. Not at all.

I hated David and loved him and was jealous of his boyfriends. Nan's voice echoed faintly in my ear: *You must take the bitter with the sweet, Francis.* My old Nan was tough, and she made me practical. While a jealous scene might be just the ticket, delicious at the moment and opening possibilities for an even more delightful reconciliation, I had a forged Picasso; a corpse in Goldfarber's studio; a blackmailing police commissioner; and, in Richard, trouble up on the Mountain. I needed to find a hiding place for the canvas, preferably immediately.

My studio was no good. David's house wasn't ideal, either, but I didn't have a lot of options. When an ignoble jealousy suggested that since he was the reason for this particular pickle, it was only fair he share the risks, I considered the room. Square and whitewashed, it sported the requisite tiled floor and wooden shutters, but no convenient closet or lockable armoire. There was a sagging green sofa, a couple of carved chairs, and the room's sole beauty, a Berber rug, all reds and earth tones, that David had hung from a thick pole.

I went into the kitchen for a hammer and a couple of small nails. I lifted the pole off its hooks and put two nails into the plaster behind where the rug would hang. I balanced the "Picasso" on the nails, replaced the rug, and stepped back. The rug hung straight and smooth, nicely covering the canvas beneath.

Once again, I was tempted to make a scene or at least to leave a message. I was mentally composing something both witty and scathing before I came to my senses. I put away the hammer and slipped out of the house. I had two hundred pounds in my pocket, and, given how quickly I can burn through money, I decided to hit the cafes immediately. After the events of the day, I needed a drink in the worst possible way, and I wanted to find some thirsty journalists willing to gossip about murder.

Soon I was combining business with liquid pleasure. Jock Fergusson wrote for the *Gazette & Mail*. "Everything of interest to the British colony: our motto and our mission," he said, though he'd be the first to admit that cricket scores and gossip were the paper's lifeblood. Jock had driven a Crusader tank in North Africa and developed a surprising affection for the desert, as well as a deep and—as far as I could see—unquenchable thirst.

"Would the British colony be interested in a murder?" I asked him. We were getting confidential in an out-of-the-way Spanish bar—small, dirty, and cheap. In the background, an aging Flamenco singer wailed about love's sorrows and life's regrets as if she'd had plenty of experience. Between her and the hard-drinking clientele, it was about as private a place as one could find in the city.

"They love a murder," Jock said. "Bred in the British bones, you ken. They love mysterious murders the best and gruesome ones next best, but only if the victim is British. We don't give a line to a native's killing. With other nationals, it's a judgment call."

Jock had a red face and a W. C. Fields nose. After a particular liquid indulgence, he had difficulties with certain consonants, but his eyes stayed cool and cynical. Even half-pickled, he was sharp. I just had to discover what I needed before he reached the full-pickled state, which he described as "reaching the Empty Quarter." Jock did like a desert metaphor.

"This was a Spaniard."

He made a little gesture with his hands. "Not quite a native but definitely not British."

"Little more than a boy," I said. "Someone cut his throat. That's the story, anyway."

Jock perked up at this. "The story, huh. From whom?"

"Our esteemed new police commissioner."

"Really." He glanced around the bar with a dubious air. "You meet him around here?"

"I met him in his office. To make a long story short—"

"Professionally speaking, I like a long story . . ."

"You're getting the short version. He's been after me to find out more about the man he thinks employed the boy."

"Really, Francis. You move in interesting circles. And you just a visitor to our fair city."

"The boy was apparently regularly employed touching up dirty pictures. That ring a bell?"

He made a show of consulting his whiskey, and I signaled for the barman to top up the glass. "Well," Jock said after a minute, "there's Calloux. His specialty is little boys and girls in tasteful shades of gray. I've heard he has to retouch in color for the modern market. Possibly the boy worked there, though I doubt it. Calloux's an artisan of the old school, half genius, half pervert, and he takes pride in his craftsmanship. Anyway, even the newest police commissioner would know about Calloux. His studio is one of the landmarks of the town for those of a certain taste." He made a face. "Personally, I draw the line at children."

"Like all good men," I said. "But you would have known if a boy had been murdered?"

"A European boy? Probably. But one of the beach boys or other native children . . ." Jock shrugged. "Considering the level of general misery, there isn't really much violence, but people do disappear. They go back to the Rif, back to the desert, down to the bottom of the sea; who knows. In hungry times, children are especially fragile."

Something in his voice made me think that he'd maybe lost a child and that it was not just bad war memories and a taste for the desert that had brought him to the *Gazette & Mail*. "Could you ask around, Jock? Your professional colleagues, maybe? Is there anyone in the Spanish Zone you could contact?"

"Aye, there's where you'd have to ask. No Spanish, have you?"

I shook my head. "Not enough."

"I'll see what I can do. And try Bernard Vallotton at *Le Journal*. Being a daily, they have a lot more columns to fill, making them a less discriminating market, if you know what I mean," Jock said and winked.

I did. *Le Journal* had a fair bit of actual world news. Jock and I drank long enough to come within sight of the Empty Quarter, but I learned nothing else. I really didn't have too many hopes of his French colleague, but the next day I called Monsieur Vallotton and invited him for lunch.

I like a good lunch. I like fish prepared by a real French chef and nicely cooked vegetables and Moroccan salads and as much Chablis or champagne as I can afford. The journalist turned out to share my tastes, and while the little cafe was unprepossessing, it had a French cook. Bernard Vallotton, pale, thin as a greyhound, and dressed in a fine, if rumpled, gray wool suit and an open-necked shirt, was favorably impressed.

He sampled his salad and nodded his head, which was decidedly expressive in an angular fashion and topped with thick brown hair cut en brosse. "This is the coming thing, you know, monsieur."

"Call me Francis," I said.

"Francis, most certainly. The coming thing in cuisine will be a fusion of French and foreign. *La belle cuisine* will conquer the postwar world, I'm convinced, but with tasteful local additions like this delightful salad. Don't you agree?"

I did. Agreement is so pleasant *en francais*; the language has so many ways of being agreeable without necessarily committing one to anything. Even better, Bernard Vallotton was originally from Paris, and since I'd learned my French there, we were getting on famously. The French have a proprietary interest in vowels and nasals as well as cuisine.

Bernard was a real gourmet. He discussed the freshness of the fish and pronounced it excellent. "It was surely swimming in the Med this morning, Francis."

I thought that very likely.

The sauce also met his approval and led to an enthusiastic conference with the waiter. Was there not a dash of cumin? And cinnamon, too! Most interesting! He emphasized his points with pale, boney hands, every finger stained brown with nicotine. It was several minutes before he let the waiter go and turned his attention back to me. "*Merveilleux.* As I was saying, Francis, a touch of the exotic within the traditional. We cannot be hidebound. *La cuisine* is a living thing."

And so on. It took a respectable tart with cheese on the side and many compliments for the perspicacity and range of *Le Journal*'s coverage before I managed to steer the conversation to homicide.

"I am surprised, Bernard, that perhaps—just perhaps, now—your fine journal missed a murder a little while ago."

He raised his eyebrows, and his black eyes turned chilly. I could see that he was as serious about journalism as he was about *la belle cuisine*. "This cannot be. If you had said yesterday, maybe. But a while ago? Impossible."

"My feeling, of course, but here's the thing." I unfolded a much-edited story about the young Spaniard with his throat cut. "He's said to have been a painter, employed in retouching photos or maybe paintings."

"Retouching paintings covers many sins." Vallotton ran a hand through his thick, dark hair and nodded for emphasis.

"I couldn't agree more. But Tangier doesn't have many galleries and photo shops. You would surely know them all."

"I would. And the killing of a worker in one of them would be news."

"And the story in *Le Journal* the next morning?"

"*Absolument.*"

"Am I to think that the photo was faked?"

"By our Zone gendarmes? Who knows with *les flics* today. We have troubled times, Francis, between bomb-throwing Moroccans and the colons' *Presence Francais* thugs. But there is another possibility—that the photo is real but the killing occurred elsewhere."

I was not sure that made me feel any better; the murder of a painter never puts me in good humor. "Where would be a likely place?"

Bernard lifted his bony shoulders and gave an eloquent shrug. "There is a powerful amount of smuggling in and out of the International Zone. Fast boats go out every night from Tangier to the Spanish Zone, and cargo comes in from the desert of the French Zone. Smuggling has been a way of life here for generations, and now with Istiqlal, it is considered a patriotic duty."

I must have looked puzzled because he added, "To deprive French customs of revenue, of course. In the hope that France will return the king and pull out of Morocco. As if we were a nation of shopkeepers—no offense intended, Francis—that cares only for money. France is, first to last, animated by *la gloire!*"

I thought money talked with most French, too, but it didn't seem the moment to say so. "What about Istiqlal?"

"Istiqlal would like patriots to concentrate on arms and grenades and material for the revolution. Poor fools! Most Moroccans just want to make a killing on cigarettes or liquor or whatever commands the price of the moment. So there can be conflicts. Smugglers have wound up dead for one reason or another."

"Spaniards, too?"

"Most certainly. There was a case in the Spanish Zone not long ago. It's possible the boy you mention was killed there. I could tell if I saw the photo."

"The photo is beyond my reach. But would your paper have a photograph of the dead smuggler?"

"I could look," said Bernard. "Could there be a story for me?"

Now it was my turn to shrug. "What about pictures, paintings? Any point in smuggling them in—or out?"

"There's not a huge market. I notice even Goldfarber's gallery is only open sporadically."

"It must be difficult for him to make a living," I said cautiously.

"Are we speaking of him? As the boy's employer?" Bernard was quick on the uptake. No Empty Quarter for him. I reminded myself to be careful.

"That is one theory. From what you've just told me, I now think it unlikely."

"You are wrong there, my friend. Herr Goldfarber has his fingers in a lot of different things."

"Including smuggling?"

"I hear that he's interested wherever there's money to be made. And he must have some other source of income, because while the gallery does not seem busy, it remains open with what I'm told is some good stock."

"A mixed bag," I said, "but, yes, some fine things, too. All prewar."

"War loot, most likely. Probably why the Jews don't trust him, though he is one of their own, and the community is famously close-knit. I find that interesting, don't you?"

I could only agree.

"And he has, shall we say, interesting friends."

I thought about the cafe beneath the studio. "He certainly has a studio for 'retouching' paintings in an interesting building."

"Where?"

I mentioned the address.

Bernard perked up. I'd clearly told him something that he did not know. "Right above one of the hotbeds of the revolution! That cafe is popular with Istiqlal as well as with some small freelance groups. They're mostly hot air here at the moment, but they've been lethal in Casablanca and Marrakech and the outlying areas."

"Reason enough for Goldfarber to attract the attention of the police?"

"One would think. But so far no one is too sure what his game is. It extends beyond the gallery. I'm certain of that."

"You might look into that studio," I said. I dared not say more. The longer it took the police to discover the dead man, the better for me. The young Spaniard was another matter. His killing had indirectly made me useful to the police, and I wanted to know more about him. "If you were to find a photo—I mean of the young man killed in the Spanish Zone—could you let me know? Could I possibly see it?"

"I don't see why not. We might walk off this excellent lunch and check at the office now. What do you say?"

I signaled the waiter. "I am in your debt, Bernard."

"Wait and see if I can find the photo," he said.

That was how I came to spend an afternoon in the smoky office of *Le Journal*, a building permeated by the smell of ink and cigarettes and filled with the clicking of typewriters, the clatter of linotype machines, and the bells of the teletypes that signaled breaking news. Bernard led me down a narrow staircase to the "morgue," where the paper's clippings rested in green metal cabinets or in brown folders arrayed along the shelves and heaped in unstable piles on the big worktable.

I doubted he would be able to find anything, but *Le Journal* clearly had a system. Bernard moved confidently along one shelf, checking the minuscule date labels, then selected a bulging accordion file and set it on the table. "Three weeks ago," he said as he drew out a story. "Your French extends to reading?"

"A little slower than in English, but yes."

"Very well. You might want to read over this week of stories. The pictures are too small to be useful, but here are the original photos."

He laid a couple of glossy eight-by-elevens on the table. One showed a square-faced young man with high cheekbones, a wide brow, and a thin, straight nose. His closed eyes were beginning to sink into the darkness of the skull; his teeth were beginning to emerge from the shrinking flesh: a morgue shot and, I thought, a painting in embryo. *Don't be distracted, Francis.* He had the same black hair, all right, quite long, and a stained white cloth was wrapped around his throat. My immediate impression was that he looked neither Spanish nor Moroccan, but I recognized the second photo immediately: it showed the "Spanish boy" lying face down in a pool of dark liquid.

I tapped the photo. "This is the same picture."

"Careless of them. They assumed that you would not double-check."

"Yes," I said. The carelessness of the powers that be is an article of faith with me, but I had another, more disagreeable thought. Maybe the commissioner and Richard, too, had anticipated that I would come to a bad end like the Spanish boy. Just the same, there must have been some reason for selecting this photo when there were surely others. "Could he really be connected in any way to Goldfarber?"

"I have no opinion. Read the stories and tell me what you think."

I began with a short piece headlined *Sordid Killing in the Spanish Zone*. Quite predictably, *Le Journal*'s writer had focused on smuggling as a possible angle. The victim, Julio Martinez, had been killed in a dive near Tetouan's port after what was described as an "altercation." The Spaniard had been carrying a Czech passport, which raised interesting questions, and he'd been employed as a housepainter, working on the decoration of what the paper described as "a large private house in the city."

I thought I'd like very much to know who owned the "large private house" as well as how Señor Martinez had acquired that Czech passport—or, alternately, given his Eastern European features, how he'd acquired documents in the name of Julio Martinez.

Later editions of *Le Journal* failed to answer these interesting questions, although I learned that the waterside tavern was a well-known haven for smugglers and that the unlucky Martinez died after a back room card game went bad. I remembered that another queer genius, Christopher Marlowe, Shakespeare's predecessor and rival, had meddled with spies and met a similar fate in a similar venue. *Mind yourself, Francis!*

But what of Martinez, himself? The paint on his clothes and hands was now easily explained. Smuggling seemed a much more likely interest for the Zone police than forged pictures. But what was he smuggling, and could paintings be involved in some way? I doubted that. Sculptures can be used to move drugs or jewels, but currency traders had easier ways to move bills than behind pictures, and with drugs, liquor, or cigarettes, bulky paintings would only be a handicap.

"There's no indication of what Martinez might have been smuggling," I said to Bernard over an aperitif later. "Is there?"

"No. I'd guess liquor or cigarettes. Ever popular and requiring no great expertise."

"Though the focus on this side seems to be the gallery." I did not mention Richard and his legation buddy and their search of the premises.

"Well," said Bernard after a moment's consideration, "there is smuggling, and then there is—what is the English phrase—washing of money."

"*Laundering*. We say, laundering money."

"Ah, same idea."

"I thought all money was clean in Tangier."

Bernard laughed. "There's something in that. But perhaps politicians are involved. All money is the same to them, but they sometimes like to hide its origin."

CHAPTER SIX

In the desert, it might have been different, but in the damp, sea-side climate of Tangier, the corpse in Goldfarber's studio was soon discovered. Bernard Vallotton, ever alert for a story, had visited the day after we met, and his keen nose detected something amiss even from the stairwell. He called the police. The next morning *Le Journal* had a front-page headline: *Mystery Corpse Discovered Above Cafe Blanco.*

The body was described as a European male in his forties, well nourished and healthy, with no distinguishing marks, and carrying no documents. He had a broken neck, which gave me a little shiver, remembering Goldfarber's meaty hand on the back of mine. I did well to escape that storage closet, for if he'd come back, I'd probably be lying in the Tangier morgue beside the mystery man.

The temporary mystery man, that is. The European sector of

the city was no larger than a big village and almost as closely knit. Within a day, he'd been identified as Jonathan Angleford, a forty-three-year-old former research chemist, writer, and student of Moroccan poetry. He was known among the expats of the Zone as an entertaining host, the provider of more than usually potent *majoun*—the cannabis-laced candy of the region—and as a font of information on Moroccan customs.

"A terrible thing," David said to me. He was getting ready for the wake, where all the Zone was expected. "He was a harmless man, all wrapped up in the poetry he was translating. He had a nice singing voice, too. He used to sing sometimes when I played at the Meridian. Really a shame."

"The Cafe Blanco, though. That's a bit dodgy, yes?"

"Full of fanatical young Moroccans, but where else would you find their poets? No, the rumors are unconscionable."

"But do tell me," I said.

"Not as I'm a gentleman." Have I mentioned that David is the soul of honor when sober? "Surely a man can attend Cambridge without becoming suspect for one thing or another."

"Surely." But I thought I would like to see what Richard thought about that, and I'd like to know the commissioner's opinion, too, although I'd avoided him since giving a highly edited account of my last meeting with Goldfarber. "He paid me off," I told him. "In full no less. I think I'm finished."

"And the painting?" the commissioner asked in his leaden voice.

"I didn't see it in the gallery. It must still be at the studio."

"We'll keep in touch. Come in sometime and you can collect that warrant."

You can be sure I wasted no time doing that, although I knew full well that the commissioner could secure another one anytime he wanted. David needed to get his assault case settled and return

to England, but I saw no chance of broaching the subject immediately. He was genuinely upset about Jonathan Angleford, who'd
been a closer, better friend than I'd realized.

"Come with me," he said. "It's going to be a difficult business."

I wasn't sure I wanted to do that, having already viewed the
deceased.

"And Edith will appreciate a good turnout."

"Edith?"

"His widow. A very nice woman, and totally devoted to Jonathan. She's interested in the arts, too. You'll like her, Francis. One of
your interesting females whom you'll disfigure in paint."

David proved right. Everyone who was anyone in the foreign colony appeared for the wake, along with a cadre of young-
ish Moroccan novelists with wary eyes and Western dress, and
older, sad-faced Moroccan poets in threadbare white djellabas,
Angleford's literary colleagues and collaborators. The Americans
were represented, too, poets and authors whom I knew in one way
or another, all turned out surprisingly tidy and sober, as well as
enough of our own scribbling countrymen to show the flag.

The Moroccans nibbled *majoun* from a big silver platter, and
the infidels laid waste to the drinks trays, while the late Jonathan
Angleford lay in state on a platform under a stained glass window.
I didn't want to renew our acquaintance, and I avoided the open
casket until David said, "Come meet Mrs. Angleford," and led me
over to the flower-banked bier.

Edith Angleford, tall, broad-shouldered, and statuesque with
jet-black hair, stood on guard beside the body, and no Praetorian
could have been more impressive. Deeply tanned and too angular
to be pretty, she had a shapely nose, straight, dark eyebrows on a
wide forehead, a thin-lipped mouth, and noble dark eyes shadowed
and swollen with sorrow. The ensemble made one of those faces,

right on the edge of caricature, whose shapes and lines you can grasp immediately. I would have picked up my brush in an instant.

She took David's hand, and he said all the right things: our regret, her sorrow, the need to be strong. Then he introduced me. She thanked me for coming, her voice low and rather hoarse, cured with cigarettes and throttled by emotion. "If I only knew why," she said to David. "If I only knew why. I can't get my mind around it."

"It's unbelievable," he said. "Completely unbelievable, though Tangier is changing." This was the local euphemism for the Moroccan independence movement, and Mrs. Angleford picked up on it instantly.

"It wasn't a Moroccan," she said sharply, "no matter where he was found. I'll never believe that. Jonathan went safely everywhere in the city, and you see his many friends here." She glanced around the room. "And," in a lower tone, "he was not killed above that cafe."

David looked surprised.

"The police as much as said so. They can tell apparently. They searched our flat." Her eyes went dead at the memory. "As if . . . as if . . . " She couldn't continue, and David put his arm around her shoulders. She recovered after a minute and shook her head. "He was my life," she said.

Though I'm skeptical of big, romantic statements, recent experiences had changed my perspective. I believed her, and perhaps that is why I took leave of my senses and bounced from one folly to the next. We were departing with the gang of transatlantic poets when she appeared at my side and laid her hand on my arm. I stopped and fell behind the others.

"Come and see me," she said. "Please, will you do that?" She slipped a piece of paper into my pocket. "My address and phone number. But you needn't bother to call ahead," she added in a bitter voice. "Where would I be now but at home?"

"All right," I said. "If I can do anything to help you, of course . . ."

She did not wait to hear my reservations and conditions but strode away across the room in her black dress, her heels aggressive on the tiles. I caught up with David and the poets, and we spent the rest of the evening in the Petite Socco, talking about Jonathan Angleford and applying liquid erasers to the disagreeable images of his dead, painted skin and shrunken carcass. I really wanted to forget the whole business, and maybe I would have but for a bad day at the easel.

I'd slashed yet another failed *Pope*, too fed up with the effort even to pass the canvas on to my needy painter friend. I was fumbling in my pocket for a pencil to sketch out yet another attempt at the pontiff, when I pulled out Edith Angleford's note. Their house was at the entrance to the Casbah, no more than a brisk walk from my studio. I hesitated for a moment, resisting obligation and entanglements. I doubted I could give her any help, but her image was so vivid in my mind that I decided it would do me no harm artistically to see her extraordinary face again.

The house, a pretty, white dwelling that caught the sea breeze and some of the perfume of the city's effluent, was set into the wall of the Casbah. I knocked on the door, half-hoping that she would be out or that my visit would be inopportune. No such luck. The door opened so quickly that she might have been waiting just behind it. Edith Angleford was all in black: black sweater and black slacks, black hair, and black eyes with black circles underneath them. Her mood looked black, too, suitable for a tragic heroine in modern dress.

"Come in, Mr. Bacon. I knew I would see you again." Her severe features lightened just a trifle.

"You must have second sight," I joked, "because I was not sure I would."

"Some say I do." She had a particularly piercing gaze. I have no truck with spirits, except bottled, but I had the unpleasant feeling that she knew more than I'd expected. More than I did, probably, although I had seen her husband under the tarp in the studio and perhaps had heard him in the gallery.

"This is a wonderful house," I said when we were settled with drinks up on the roof terrace. I was quite taken with the architecture, which was spare, white, and solid, suitable for a monk's cell or a poet's roost. The decor was minimal, too, with only a few bright rugs, some framed photos, including one of Jonathan in full Moroccan kit, and a shelf of Edith Angleford's silver skeet-shooting trophies.

Personally, I tend to work in clutter; the casual juxtapositions possible in a blizzard of papers and books and paints and photographs can be suggestive. Perhaps that is why I have difficulty working away from home, where the mulch of years litters the studio floor. Just the same, I can admire the clean, tidy, and ascetic that's really more to David's taste than mine.

Edith shook her head. "It's lovely in the summer but green with mold all winter."

"The curse of seaside places. I'm a city man myself."

"What are you doing in Tangier?"

I shrugged. "Like the song: 'The Man I Love.'"

She smiled then, a tourist in the foreign land of disaster who has spotted a fellow countryman. "I knew I wasn't mistaken in you."

"And you, will you stay in Tangier now?" I asked quickly. She made me uneasy, and I wanted to postpone any revelations.

Edith looked away over the jumbled cityscape with its white walls, its faded awnings, and flat roofs: a cubist pile with a severely geometric squalor. "For the moment, maybe for always, but certainly until I find out what happened to Jonathan."

"They say that the new police commissioner is very competent."

"They say a lot of things. Few of them are true."

"Especially in Tangier?"

"Most especially here."

There was a pause. I waited. The wine was good, and I ate some of the dates she'd laid out on a little yellow dish. She remained silent so long that finally, I asked her what she thought I could do to help.

She fixed me with her large eyes, dark, sad, a little mad, too. I recognized the territory. "Tell me what happened," she said.

"The police say," I began, but she shook her head.

"I know what they say. I want to know what *you* say."

"I didn't know your husband, although David did. I just came to the wake to keep him company."

"I didn't think you would lie to me," she said.

Naturally, I tried to bluff my way and obscure the issue. I'm rather a good liar, and most of the time I find lying easy because other people are dishonest or hedging the truth in turn. Edith was having none of it.

She interrupted me, "Shall I tell you how I know?"

"It will be news to me," I said.

"You were the only one at the wake not to look at Jonathan. The only one. If you really didn't know him, you would be curious and indifferent. But you were not indifferent, and you were not curious."

An unsettling degree of observation under the circumstances! I told her I had a dislike of the dead, of seeing the dead, but she had an answer to this lame suggestion.

"Then you wouldn't have come. And your paintings—oh, yes, I've seen them and admired them, too—suggest you are not so squeamish."

She had me there, and I considered what I could tell her that would be both true and safe. "Let me ask you something first. Who was your husband working for?"

"What do you mean?"

"How did he make his living?"

I thought that her face clouded just a little. "He inherited a modest sum. With his writing and translating and my teaching at the American school, we lived here quite comfortably. By our standards, anyway. Unlike most of the expats, we didn't expect luxury."

"Could I ask when he received his inheritance?"

"I don't know what that has to do with anything," she said, clearly annoyed.

She thought I was stalling, and I was, but not entirely. "I don't know what might be important," I said. "So I'm asking about everything."

I half-expected her to refuse—more people balk at confiding their finances than their sex lives—but she said, "Just after he left Cambridge, as a matter of fact. It enabled us to get married."

That sounded like a very nice coincidence, although such things do happen, and rich aunts and uncles sometimes die in a timely fashion. But sometimes, too, bright university boys get themselves onto mysterious payrolls.

"Did he know a man named Goldfarber?"

"The owner of that local gallery, you mean? No more than I did. Although we went to a couple of openings, Jonathan didn't really approve of Herr Goldfarber."

"No?" That was interesting, although I suspected that, on closer acquaintance, most people wouldn't approve of the art dealer.

"Jonathan was suspicious about how the Goldfarber Gallery acquired its stock. There was a little Matisse etching I wanted to buy, but he wouldn't let me. He was desperately idealistic, you understand." She bit her lip. "He wanted the world to be a better place. He thought, he really thought, that change for the better was possible. He had such faith," she said, seizing my hand. "Such enormous faith."

I am always half-frightened of idealists, who can justify any monstrosity, but I felt the force of her belief. Whatever her husband had or had not been, she believed in *him*. That undoubtedly made her a fool, but who was I to mock the follies of love? She thought her husband was wonderful, and there were days when I thought David was a prince. I knew better; maybe she did, too. "I believe he went to see Goldfarber on the day he died," I said.

"For what reason?" I heard a sharp anxiety in her voice. "Why?"

"I don't know. Goldfarber owed me money, and as it happened when I arrived, I was wearing a burnoose. Such as your husband sometimes wore?"

She nodded. "He always said that the locals anywhere know best how to dress. And a gesture of solidarity, too." Suddenly, her eyes grew wet. "Not that they appreciated, particularly. To them, he was an eccentric infidel and to the expats, a doubtful compatriot as you can imagine."

I could, indeed. Edith Angleford's life in Tangier could not have been particularly easy, caught between an idealistic husband and not one, but two materialistic communities.

"I'd been shopping in the souk that day, and I picked up a burnoose as a souvenir. The wind was cold, and I put it on before I reached the gallery. Goldfarber had obviously been waiting for someone. He opened the door, but he was upset when he saw who it was. He tried to throw me right out, and he was nervous enough to pay me so I'd leave right away."

"Why is this important?" she asked. She did both hostility and skepticism superbly well.

"Because I think it was your husband he was waiting for. He

saw the burnoose and assumed I was Jonathan." I gave her a brief summary of what had transpired in the gallery. With even a much-edited account, I risked either incriminating myself or looking totally ridiculous. I'd like to know why serious events in my life so often include an element of farce.

Edith zeroed right in on that. "You let Goldfarber lock you in a closet?"

"I thought it was the back door."

She stared at me for a moment. She had a good stare; I thought I'd like to see her square off against the commissioner. "But then he let you out?"

"No, he never came back. Maybe he hasn't yet. I was left to starve," I said, but she was not interested in my fate. "Fortunately, I got out. I had a look around the gallery and the office, where I saw some drops of blood."

"And Jonathan lying dead! I knew it, I knew it. That horrible man killed him."

"Probably," I said. "But whatever had happened—and I can't tell you more because the walls are so thick that I heard nothing definite—both were gone by the time I left the closet."

"You saw his body." Her flat voice carried absolute conviction. She had a remarkably forceful personality, and yet I was almost convinced that a big part of her husband's life had been closed to her.

"Not at the gallery, Edith. Not there."

She leaped up in great distress. "Oh, God, you went to the studio and you didn't call the police!"

"I did ensure that he would be discovered."

"Listen to yourself! *Ensured he'd be discovered!* What sort of man are you? A day late! More than a day late. You can't imagine how I felt! How I worried! For years, we were never apart more than a day or two. And he lay there a whole day and night. Rotting in this stinking damp."

She was right. I had no justification except necessity, which is an exceedingly flexible concept. "You asked me what happened. I have told you," I said, standing up.

"And now you wash your hands and leave," she said bitterly.

"Remember that I'm a visitor here with no stake in anything. I've told you what I know at some risk to myself. "

"And I am insufficiently grateful," she said sarcastically. I recognized Edith Angleford as a connoisseur of big scenes and high emotions. And strong will, too, for she was struggling to control herself. Her voice dropped several decibels, and she asked, "But you are sure about Goldfarber?"

"As sure as I can be."

She nodded and bit her lip and looked out over the streets of the Casbah and down toward the medina. I wondered what she really thought of Tangier, of Morocco, of Moroccans.

"What will you do now?" I asked.

"I will search for Herr Goldfarber," she said immediately in a cold, flat voice.

"He's a large, powerful, dangerous man. I wouldn't recommend that."

"I'm not going to date him," she said. "I'm going to kill him.

CHAPTER SEVEN

In theory, Edith Angleford's idea had a lot of appeal, but I could see big problems for her in practice. And maybe for me, too, because, although we parted on bad terms, I had a suspicion that sooner or later the vengeful widow would see a way either to enlist my help or to put me in danger. In short, my visit was a neat illustration of the perils of good intentions. Despite that nice Spanish red on the Angleford roof terrace, I found myself irresistibly drawn to a dive in the Socco, where I set a resolute course for the Empty Quarter. I was well on my way when David appeared, looking fitter and happier than he had in weeks, if not months. His face was shining, his hair brushed, his clothes, impeccable.

"Francis! What are you doing here? Today needs an elegant cafe and good champagne!"

His greeting should have warned me, but it was such a pleasure to see him happy that I was content in the moment. I paid my tab and joined him for a late, and quite splendid, lunch.

"No, my treat," he said when I tried to pay. "I've come into money. Not real money, you understand, but sufficient unto the day, unto fines and lawyers, and certain niggling overdue bills."

"That's wonderful," I said. I told myself that it was just my recent proximity to the Empty Quarter and my visit to Edith Angleford that suddenly made me apprehensive. "Your case is settled? So quickly?"

"A man with a sharp lawyer can do wonderful things, especially in Tangier. Money is so eloquent here."

"Congratulations. I imagine that you'll be making plans to leave the Zone. There's no reason now for you to stay, is there?"

"No reason?" He gave a wicked smile. "Let me count the ways: Khalid, Bilal, Ali, Jamal . . . Why would I ever want to leave?"

Why, indeed? He was playful, but I was serious. We had drifted apart, and Tangier was proving dangerous for my health, not to mention my painting. "So why did you ask me, beg me, actually, to visit?"

"I missed you, of course. You suffer, and I enjoy." He showed his teeth and gave a sly grin.

Once, my heart would have beat faster. Now, I wasn't in the mood. "I could be in London, where I can paint. I could be getting ready for a show and repaying the loans from my gallery. I wouldn't have come if you hadn't asked me."

His face changed. Perhaps only long acquaintance enabled me to register his emotions, but I suspected that he had lost some psychic armor. Military discipline had worn away with high, or more exactly low, living, and I could see that his new cheerfulness was only skin-deep. "I was in a bad way," he said. "And you understand me."

"Now you're in a good way and determined to stay. Perhaps Khalid, Bilal, Ali, or Jamal will prove to be understanding in time."

It was a mistake to sound bitter with David. He liked to be in control and provoke reactions. I understood, but I was losing patience with the game.

"I'm counting on it. Besides, where have you been lately?"

No point in discussing that. David was proud and touchy; knowing my efforts on his behalf would be deeply humiliating for him. And there are times when one needs to know the worst immediately. This was one of them. "How did you come into money? A late rich relative?"

Again the sly grin. "No, something far better in a way. I was with Abdullah. Or was it Karim? No matter. Things were progressing and then"—he darkened slightly—"too much kef or too much wine produced a misunderstanding and led to—"

"I don't need all the details," I said. If David didn't leave Tangier, he'd be right back in the commissioner's clutches.

"Oh, but you'll be interested. Leading, as I said, to frolics in the living room, leading to pillows and lamps thrown, before a certain handsome Berber rug was ripped from the wall, producing a fine surprise."

"Right. You found the 'Picasso.'" My heart sank. The only saving grace was that Abdullah or Karim or the boy of the moment had not made off with it. "The painting's a fake, of course."

"By your fine hand, I'd guess. Much the best thing you've ever done, Francis. Why you labor on the rubbish you produce when you might live in luxury beggars the imagination."

"What did you do with it, David?"

"I sold it, of course. I hadn't realized what a marketable item good art is. It was no bother at all. I went out with it under my jacket and came back with a thousand pounds. But you don't seem happy. Thanks to your work, I'm a free man, unencumbered legally, and once again a respectable member of Tangierino society—if that isn't a contradiction in terms."

He sounded breezy and lighthearted; it pained me to think that forgery had produced this improvement, as if the way to his heart was through dodgy pictures. Though someone like Edith Angleford might sacrifice all for love, this idea gave me pause. "Who bought it, David?"

"Wouldn't you like to know," he teased.

"It's more a matter of needing to know," I said. "But I have a good idea in any case."

"I'm sure you do. Who collects Picassos? Real or otherwise? Why our good friend Richard. One glance and he had to have it."

I bet he did. "He didn't ask where you'd gotten it? He never questioned its provenance?"

"You know, Francis, I think our friend's expertise is much exaggerated. You had to clue him in about the first painting. If you'd had your wits about you, you'd have said it was one hundred percent Spanish Master and sold him a gallery full."

I got up from the table, grabbed the edge of the cloth, and tipped dishes, cutlery, wine glasses, carafes, and coffee cups into his lap. "I was never an officer and a gentleman like you, but I'm no hack. And don't get up or I'll flatten you." I turned so quickly that I knocked my chair onto the floor. I stepped over it, shoved the waiter, and headed straight for the door. David's voice rose behind me, but his every word was incinerated by anger.

I stormed down the narrow lane to the market square, squeezing past shoppers and overloaded donkeys, dodging ancient trucks and fancy cars. I'd been a fool to come, a fool to involve myself in David's troubles, a fool to stay one minute more in the wretched, seductive, filthy, beautiful city. I would pack my things, buy a ticket for the ferry, and be in Spain tomorrow. I love excess, I really do, but even the most intense pleasures can wear thin. David was beginning to exceed my emotional exchequer, and I wanted to get out before my account was overdrawn.

In this determined mood, I climbed the stairs to my studio, my mind full of resolution and exciting new images. I can't paint around David; there's too much turmoil and drama, but there's no doubt that the aftermath is inspiration. Given my habits, it's probably no surprise that *my* Muse is an alcoholic sadist with deadly charm. *Chacun à son goût!* But no longer. Propelled by good intentions and common sense, I put the key in the door of my studio and found it already unlocked. A little carelessness on my part?

Yes, I decided, and opened the door. Wrong: two men had made themselves comfortable in my chairs. Even against the light, I recognized Richard and next to him, a blond head. Clearly I had proven irresistible to my friend from the medina.

"Come in," said Richard. "We took the liberty."

"You took too much liberty," I said sourly. "I let very few people into my studio." I was more than annoyed, I was semipanicked. Richard was a weasel, cozy with the police commissioner and attached to some mysterious outfit at the legation. His arrival could only be bad news.

"A thousand pardons for invading the sanctity of the studio."

Where does the damn old queen get those Edwardian turns of phrase? He must study them, because he's not old enough to remember them.

"But time is of the essence," he continued. "Her Majesty's Government needs your help."

"I worked for her father during the war. It really didn't suit me. My plan at the moment is to leave Tangier on the morning ferry."

"As a friend, I would heartily recommend that. But I'm here in a different capacity."

"One that involves breaking and entering, I see."

"Alas, that has come into it." He shook his head with what might have been regret but which I took to be playacting. "We really have come for your help."

"The last time I gave you some 'help,' I wound up doing a favor for the police commissioner and working illegally for a man whom I now assume is a murderer. Not a good recommendation, Richard."

"You refer to Goldfarber?" Like a switch turned off, all the camp antics were gone.

"The same. A dangerous man, as I'm sure you and your colleague know perfectly well."

"We'd be interested in your observations," he said smoothly.

I considered whether the pleasure of surprising him outweighed the possible benefits of secrecy, but he had the painting and doubtless would collect my fingerprints. He could make trouble for me, but maybe I could make some for him. "I suspect they would overlap your own, seeing that we both visited Goldfarber's gallery the other afternoon. You and tall-blond-and-handsome here were in the gallery and in the office. I was on the stairs and eventually on top of the water tank."

Richard was clearly taken aback. "You were in the gallery. The whole time?"

"I went to collect some money. Money for the picture I understand you just bought."

"I must congratulate you on that, quite beyond what I'd have expected of you," Richard said, momentarily falling out of his role as a man of mysterious government affairs. "It puts my other 'Picasso' quite to shame. And it dried so quickly, too. Do tell me how!"

"That's a trade secret." I thought how easy it is to admire the already famous, which is how most connoisseurs get their reputations.

"And did he pay you?"

"As a matter of fact, he did. Instead of cutting my throat, which maybe you'd expected?"

Richard's face went red. "Steady on," he said. "I had nothing to do with your association with Goldfarber. I hadn't a clue that you had done work for him."

"Except for putting me in the way of the commissioner, who was investigating Goldfarber, whose previous assistant wound up dead. No, fortunately for me, Herr Goldfarber was expecting someone. Someone dressed, as I was at that moment, in a burnoose. Sound familiar?"

The blond man spoke up for the first time. "Did you see him? The visitor?"

I shook my head and described my imprisonment in the storage room, the unintelligible voices of Goldfarber and his visitor, and the sound as of something—or someone—being dragged across the gallery.

"Why didn't you answer us when we called?" Richard demanded. "If you were already freed from the closet, you must have heard us."

"I didn't know who you were, and when I did recognize your voice, I wondered what you were up to. Not your usual role, is it, Richard? Looking out for transmitters and searching offices? Speaking of that, did you notice a little blood on the desk? I hope Her Majesty's servants were alert to that. You might have called the police, and poor Jonathan Angleford might have been found more quickly."

He muttered something about "standard procedures" and "jeopardizing the operation." Given a few more minutes, I think he'd have ventured on "state secrets." In short, he covered his backside as I'd covered mine; I guess the secret services are human after all. "Best not let Mrs. Angleford know," I said. "Until her husband's killer is found, she's going to make life difficult for all Bad Samaritans."

I thought he seemed momentarily distressed; whatever else he was—and his identity appeared to be both interesting and complicated—Richard really was enthralled with his place in Tangierino society.

"Well, we will have to produce Goldfarber, won't we? It will be in everyone's interest: the commissioner's, ours, Mrs. Angleford's, and yours."

"I will applaud from afar," I said. "From my London studio, to be exact. And now, gentlemen, I must pack."

I made this announcement with a considerable show of confidence, but Richard didn't move and neither did his companion. The possibility of social complications had been my best card, and Richard was going to leave it on the table. "We have a plan," he said, "to flush him out."

I didn't like the sound of that. Even the verb was ill-chosen.

"We believe that he is in the Spanish Zone."

"Why?"

Richard and his companion exchanged glances. "What I tell you now is highly confidential, classified information."

"Best to leave me out of it, then. I have security risk written all over me."

"We considered that," Richard said sourly. "However, you seem curiously blackmail-proof."

"Candor has its uses, gentlemen."

"No doubt. You are vulnerable on only one point."

I felt my chest prickle, preliminary to seizing up; I knew what was coming.

"That fine—shall we call it a 'Picasso homage'—might be misconstrued. Not here, certainly. Here in Tangier, its creation was a very public spirited act, admirable even. But London's a different matter, don't you know. I've always found the London art world catty, even vicious."

This was true. It was also true that I hate lying in paint and that forgery is one of the rare accusations that could both embarrass and injure me. I should have taken Nan's advice, avoided passion, and stuck with rich gents from Mayfair.

"Fortunately," Richard said, "I am in possession of the doubtful item. I can keep it as an amusing souvenir to test would-be connoisseurs' acumen. Or I could consign it to the flames."

"Much the best thing," I said.

"I agree. But Her Majesty's Government has a thousand pounds invested in the work, and there will be problems accounting for it without some profit to us."

"There might be questions raised about how you failed to find Angleford's body, too," I said, determined to go down on the attack. "And why you apparently ignored the evidence in his office."

"That might be so, theoretically," said Richard, "but there won't be any questions."

Definitely a hint of menace. Could I have been mistaken about who killed the Spanish boy? Even Angleford? No, not Angleford; I had heard a large object being dragged across the gallery floor. That was surely Goldfarber's doing.

"The operation we are engaged in is important. Important for us, for Tangier, for the future of North Africa." Richard sounded ready to address the House of Lords.

"A lot of people have ideas for the future of North Africa," I remarked. I detest politics and tend to reduce all issues to the personal. Nadir with his lacerated back and his curious bracelet and his faithful friends seemed admirable in a way that neither the commissioner nor Richard was. Whatever the wild Berbers came up with could hardly be worse than the corrupt mess of the Zone.

"The Soviets are interested in stirring up trouble," Richard continued. "They want to use Moroccan anger over the king's exile to promote a Marxist government in the region. With Gibraltar just across the straits, Her Majesty's Government cannot allow that. And will not."

"And you assume that Goldfarber was a Soviet agent of some sort?" Apparently agents came in all shapes and sizes, but an art dealer with a sideline in forged paintings seemed unlikely. "Wouldn't his dubious stock make him a suspect for one thing or another?"

"Exactly. He was an unreliable Soviet agent. It is likely that he killed Angleford and possibly one other associate. It might have been to hide his profitable sideline."

"But why Angleford? A British poet with an enthusiasm for Moroccan verse."

Richard looked at his colleague, who gave the slightest of nods.

"Jonathan Angleford was an enthusiast of all things Moroccan. We also have evidence that from the time he left Cambridge he was a committed Marxist and very possibly a Soviet agent."

I remembered that David had hinted at something similar with his sly references to Cambridge and the notorious spy ring. I felt a pang for Edith Angleford. "Goldfarber seems to be eliminating Soviet agents. Perhaps you should leave well enough alone."

"It's more complicated than that. Angleford was still a British subject. It would look very strange if the legation didn't take an interest, and the devoted Mrs. Angleford is ready to move heaven and earth to get his killing solved. Besides, there are Goldfarber's masters. We think we can get farther up the chain."

The whole operation had an off smell to it, and I wasn't inclined to take Richard's word for anything. "Such a delicate operation requires a professional," I said. "How you can think about involving me is beyond imagining."

"Normally," said the blond man, "we'd never give you a thought."

I believed that. He was disdainful and full of himself.

"But Goldfarber needs a painter."

"Surely not still. His sideline wrecked whatever else he was doing, didn't it?"

"For that very reason," Richard said. "He's been acting like a man who wants out. In from the cold, so to speak."

"I didn't think one resigned."

"Oh, no, no. Not from Mother Russia. But money can buy a new identity. He wants stock to sell to unwary collectors in France, England, the US, Brazil. Where can one not go with valuable artwork?"

Where indeed. "But to kill Angleford. Surely the Soviets will be furious."

"Well, exactly," said Richard. "So both Goldfarber and his controllers will be pleased to know that he did not kill Jonathan Angleford."

"Certainly, they'll be relieved," I admitted. "But there isn't much doubt, is there?"

"That's where you come in," Richard said. "There'll be just enough doubt. Don't worry about a thing. It's all arranged. The police should be here in"—he paused and consulted his watch—"twenty minutes, more or less. Just enough time for you to pack your painting kit. We took the liberty of packing your clothes; no point in cutting it too fine, old boy."

I felt as if I'd stepped into some Dadaist farce. "You want me to run away from a murder I didn't commit?"

"Correction, one you most likely did commit. Your presence in the gallery and in the studio can be documented. I wouldn't be surprised if a search of your person revealed a key to the Goldfarber studio. The commissioner is a clever man. He knows how to take a hint—and build a case."

"It would never stand up," I said, although I didn't feel totally confident. I suspected that, like everything else in the Zone, criminal cases were susceptible to pressures of one sort or another.

"We should hope not!" Richard said, with a touch of his old friendliness. "But disagreeable at the time, don't you know. Very disagreeable and apt to have lasting consequences. I wouldn't risk it personally, but the decision is up to you."

I was tempted to call their bluff, and I sat for several minutes without saying anything. Then the blond fellow took out a nasty-looking pistol. Richard started to protest, but his colleague shook his head. "He needs to be out of here, whether he cooperates or not. He's a suspect in a capital crime. It's only natural he runs. Pack up the paints," he said to me. "We have to be gone before the police arrive."

CHAPTER EIGHT

My situation was nasty. Richard was bad; the blond man, whose name was Harry, was worse—his ready familiarity with his weapon, beyond the pale. At the same time, I didn't totally believe them. The commissioner had been interested in Goldfarber from the start, and clearly Richard and Harry were convinced that the gallery dealer was a Soviet spy. I was tempted to delay, hope the police arrived, and confront them all.

Harry wasn't having that. He made a big package of stretched canvases, located a roll of nice Belgian linen, and tied up a bundle of stretchers. Richard put my paint tubes in a canvas bag. At the rate they were going, my studio would soon be emptied, and how would I work then? Admitting defeat, I folded my easel, wrapped my brushes, and boxed the bottles of turpentine and linseed oil. Every few minutes, my two visitors looked out the windows or checked the stairwell, and by the time we were ready, I'd been infected by their nerves. When Harry gestured with his revolver toward the door, I grabbed my leather coat and the canvases. Preceded by Richard with my suitcase and followed by Harry with gun and paints, I hustled downstairs.

The white Mercedes was parked around the corner. As we loaded my equipment, I wondered how far I'd get if I made a break for it. Not far enough, probably, for although the street was narrow, it was not busy. Harry looked athletic, and after the incident in the medina, he wouldn't be easy to fool a second time. The only possibility for improving my prospects was the street drain near the car. I felt in my pocket for Goldfarber's studio key. When Harry grabbed my other arm to shove me into the Mercedes, I dropped the key. It rang on the metal grate before disappearing into the unmentionable slime of the city.

"What was that?"

"Damned if I know," I said.

Harry looked around. I think he might have begun a little investigation, if Richard hadn't said, "That's surely a siren."

With that hint of the police, we were off. I expected a quick run up the Mountain and hospitality at Richard's; you can see that I still did not really understand the situation. Instead, we drove out beyond the old city walls until we reached a dismal waste of dry ground. In the distance, thin columns of smoke rose from a wooded valley with a cluster of dark tents. I could see women moving around the fires, and donkeys, horses, and camels tethered nearby: country living, Moroccan-style. I didn't like it any better than Berkshire.

Our destination was a little roadside settlement, a cluster of earthen structures, shielded by fruit trees and palms that rustled in the dry breeze. We parked beside a building a little apart from the rest. The white stucco coat was peeling and chipped, but there were stout bars on the front windows and a good lock on the garage door. Harry got out and opened it. Inside was a green van.

"Can you drive?" he asked.

Instant memories of treacherous French roads and the mysteries of the gear shift. "I have driven," I said. "It was not a success."

Harry seemed exasperated, as if someone shanghaied on a murder charge could be expected to turn his hand to anything.

"No matter," said Richard impatiently. "He can hire a driver if need be. See to that before you leave."

Harry gave a put-upon grunt and opened the back of the van to load my painting equipment.

"We'll need your passport," Richard said. "Some needful alterations, you understand."

I wasn't keen on this at all, but Harry stuck his hand into my jacket and came out with my documents. Richard immediately set to work with a small scalpel and a tube of glue. He laid my passport on the hood of the van and carefully removed the photo. Then he took another British passport and inserted my picture. Amid a flurry of control stamps and visas, I'd become Jerome Hume, artist and decorative painter.

I've acquired a number of different names in my time, but *Jerome* was a new low. A father of the church who spent his time in desert austerities was hardly my cup of tea, certainly not accompanied as he'd been by all those pious ladies without a bum boy in sight. I decided that I must take what comfort I could in *Hume*, the rationalist Scot who thought causality a mere habit of mind. I wondered if he'd worked for a secret service. Certainly he and Jerome made a very odd couple.

"It's good workmanship," Richard said, as if I might have doubts. I certainly did, but not about his phony passport. "Harry will see you over the border. Tetouan is quite nice. Near the sea, don't you know. You're an artist working away undisturbed in a charming rural setting."

"Right," I said. "The last place on earth I'd go."

"Everything's laid on," Richard said imperturbably. "And you'll notice that we've packed several books on Picasso. Pages marked with works supposed missing in the war. That's what you'll be working on."

"This is a crazy scheme. For one thing, Goldfarber will know exactly who I am."

"Of course he will. You're only Jerome Hume until you cross the border. Goldfarber needn't know how you got across. You were accused, you fled. Simple enough. Don't make unnecessary complications. And remember, old boy, inner conviction is worth more than even the best cover story."

Easy for him to say. He didn't have to convince a homicidal forger. "And why exactly am I painting fake Picassos?"

"You were inspired by the success of the one you stole. Sold it in a minute, which is perfectly true, as you'd do well to remember— on several accounts." Richard had a disconcerting way of switching between the pleasantly frivolous and the deadly serious. "Now you have legal troubles, and you need money fast."

"Why didn't I take the ferry to Gibraltar or Spain? I could have been on my way to London before anyone was the wiser."

"Don't think of it," said Richard in a cold voice. "Any attempt to leave Spanish territory would be very dangerous for you. If we cannot get Goldfarber, you would do for Angleford's killing, and leaving personal feelings aside, it would be no great matter if you were killed escaping. Keep that in mind."

Right. I'd certainly focus on that, but I rather missed the nice old Queen of Tangierino society. I hadn't appreciated him half enough until I met his alter ego, who worked with thugs and devised half-assed schemes. "You think this will bring Herr Goldfarber out of the woodwork and eager to buy forged Picassos?"

"We're counting on it," Richard said. "Tetouan is a small place and not like the Zone. You'll need to mind yourself, Francis: not too much tripping the light fantastic, if I can put it that way."

I don't think my activities have ever been described in that way, but I knew what he meant and quite rejected the idea. Getting out and about and drinking and carrying on is the breath of life to me, along with painting. I said nothing.

"News of a stranger and a painter will soon reach his ears," Richard continued.

"If he's there," I said.

"We're sure he is. Smugglers have ways of leaving Tangier without clearing customs, and the Spanish Zone was his base of operations. Besides, he had to leave most of his stock behind at the gallery, sealed and guarded as a crime scene. He won't be able to resist."

"Very nice," I said. "I'm the goat to tempt the leopard."

"No leopards here," Richard said in a fussy way, "and the poor Barbary lions are more or less extinct."

As if I cared about North African wildlife. "What happens to me if he comes, is what I'm asking. Or is that an irrelevant detail?"

"A detail of the first importance," Richard said, feigning shock. I could see that he wanted to have it both ways, to be a pillar of good society and a hard man of the secret services. "We have a man in Tetouan—very reliable, very competent. He'll be in touch. You can count on being under surveillance the whole time."

I was pretty sure that I couldn't count on anything except being, as my wicked uncle Lastings used to say, "down the rabbit hole." I had an impulse to expand on that, but Harry produced his revolver again. The firearm was rather a crutch for him, which I took as a

Freudian sign of some embarrassing personal weakness. Just the same, I got into the van.

"Good luck, old boy," said Richard, all his bonhomie restored. He got into his white Mercedes, now speckled gray and brown with dust, and drove away.

Harry closed and locked the garage and got into the van. It was not a prepossessing vehicle, and I was surprised by the smooth purr of the motor and by the powerful acceleration it revealed once we left the settlement.

Harry gave me a sly look. "American V-8 engine," he said. "Runs like a son of a bitch, but eats the petrol. Always carry a few extra cans in the back."

Apparently, either Richard or Harry knew something about motors. I wouldn't have put money on much expertise, otherwise. "Right," I said. I tried for conviction but clearly failed.

"You really can't drive?"

"I'm a London man. Londoners don't need to drive."

"I could teach you, easy," he said and patted my knee.

Oh, ho, Francis! Oh, ho! But no, definitely no. I like rough trade, and I like reckless, but there are limits. He and Richard had set me up for a murder charge, and what might that bring here? Firing squad, guillotine, hanging? Even beheading might not be off the docket. I had no idea and no Nan to enlighten me. "Hire me a driver," I said. "I fancy risking my life in style."

He laughed then. "Too bad we're on duty. My line of work, you meet a lot of interesting people."

I could agree with that. "I'm interested in Angleford, since I'm supposed to have murdered him. Did I have a reason?"

Harry made a face. "Artistic differences?" he suggested.

I noted a lack of conviction.

"No one will ask you," he said quickly. "I'd avoid the whole topic."

"Easy for you to say, but you must know something about him. He was a Soviet agent?"

"That's right."

"Not maybe working both sides?"

I got another sharp look. "What makes you think that?"

I shrugged. What I really thought was that he and Richard seemed out for revenge and much more distressed about the death of an enemy agent than I thought reasonable. What I said was, "Remember Goldfarber murdered him, not me. I thought agents who got out of line were quietly called back to Mother Russia. Isn't that the drill? Now Goldfarber is on the run and whatever he was up to is on hold or ruined. Killing Angleford was a stupid move, unless he was really dangerous."

Harry's face took on an expression of distaste. "Angleford was an idealist. A Morocco for the Moroccans type. The empire meant nothing to him. Scrap it tomorrow, was his attitude. He had useful contacts with the rebels, and we think he funneled Soviet money to Istaqlal and some other political groups."

"And Goldfarber was one link in the chain?"

"Right."

"An unhappy link."

"Probably. People got sucked into the Soviet networks during the war or were recruited afterward out of the refugee camps. The Reds were in a hurry, and not all their recruits proved to be committed Marxists."

Harry went on in this vein for some time. I learned quite a bit about the Soviet network, and the British secret service's concern about the Communist menace in North Africa. What I didn't learn was the exact status of the late Jonathan Angleford. Could he have been one of ours as well as one of theirs? And was that the real reason Harry and Richard were making such efforts to locate Goldfarber? I didn't know, and clearly Harry, despite little flirtatious gestures, was not going to tell me.

The sun was a huge red ball, sinking rapidly by the time we reached the border. Getting our visas and passports checked proved to be a dusty, dismal, nervous business. I was torn between the desire to be stamped legit and on my way, and an almost equally strong desire to be stopped and thereby extracted from Harry's clutches.

After a dignified interval, the persnickety Spanish border agents roused themselves to inspect our papers. They examined the van, too, clearly interested in the unfamiliar painting equipment.

"Mr. Hume is traveling for his health," Harry said, which in one way was indubitably true. "Looking for inspiration, right?" A glance at me.

My turn. I enlarged on the beauty of the Rif, the splendid seashore, the charm of the quaint towns with their traditional Moroccan buildings—basically all things I'd never paint and would barely notice. Meanwhile, I couldn't help eyeing a very fetching young Spaniard dressed in the whites of a Moroccan army officer. I don't normally have a yen for military finery, but he was so decorative that I began to think the Spanish Zone would have its compensations. I certainly meant to find out.

At last, satisfied that I was Jerome Hume off to paint the local scenery and that Harry was my hired driver, the customs agent stamped our documents. "You are free to travel in the Spanish Zone," he said grandly. "Welcome to Spanish Morocco."

"What did I tell you?" Harry asked as we pulled away. "A piece of cake. Best documents Her Majesty can buy."

I agreed the workmanship was superb, but I suspected that I might have waltzed across with my own papers and been welcomed just as readily. My doubts about the situation were very unpleasant. If this were all an elaborate charade, I'd have one set of feelings. If

I was really wanted for murder, I'd have another. As it was, a sinister absurdity hung over both options, and I found myself waffling between amusement and fear.

We drove south and east toward Tetouan and the coast. The quick Mediterranean night had come down, and the mountains of the Rif rose against the night sky, their peaks silvered in the moonlight. The dark foothills, furred with thorny scrub, plunged down to the flat silver sea and grayish strand, but such spectacular landscapes are not for me. The right motif calls to you—or does not. If it does, the simplest image has a wonder of ideas and implications; if it does not, no skill can redeem your work.

Tetouan was a white cubist jumble like Tangier, scarcely lit but for the string of cafes around the market area, and providing a pungent perfume for the night wind. We drove through the center and down toward the port, some kilometers away. I was to be lodged on a hilly street near the water with a "most desirable ocean view," according to Harry; perhaps he fancied another life as a rental agent. Moonlight revealed a blocky, flat-roofed house surrounded by palms and fig trees and various unfamiliar and vaguely threatening shrubs. The sleepless insects were noisy in the trees, and some late blossoms promised trouble for my asthma. I was longing for Soho before I stepped from the van.

Inside, I found a good-sized room for a studio, with a tiny kitchen and bedroom below. Apparently, the place came with an elderly Moroccan woman who would clean and see to my meals.

"No need for you to shop or go out," said Harry, who was obviously imagining my stay as a sort of artistic purdah. "She's quite deaf, too, and she knows no English. You'll be perfectly safe, and we can speak freely."

I said that was reassuring, but I thought that isolation and Harry made a most undesirable combination.

"And the gardener—one of ours," he continued as he started unloading the van. "He takes care of several gardens nearby, so he is always around."

"How can I possibly worry? Unless someone chooses to visit outside of the gardener's hours."

"He lives in a little shed at the bottom of this garden. No, I don't think you need to be nervous." Harry's expression was blandly unconcerned.

I shrugged and picked up the satchel with my oil paints. If Harry didn't see the disadvantages of the place, he was unimaginative, incompetent—or hostile. While we transferred my equipment to the makeshift studio, he explained the arrangements. He would take the van now and set up a driver, a man that the gardener could fetch when required. Everything was laid on and I need not worry about money.

I was barely listening. I set up my easel and arranged my paints on a small table along with the book of Picasso reproductions. This struck me as a very bad spot, and I thought that, despite Richard's warnings, I should get myself out of the Spanish Zone and leave North Africa as soon as possible.

CHAPTER NINE

I was eager to get rid of Harry, who spoke of "sharing a few glasses" and getting to know me. That's the sort of thing I try; I expected more focus from a man spending the Queen's shillings and guarding the realm. Besides, the light of the oil lamps was not kind to him. Blond good looks come to grief under the African sun, and close up, he reminded me strongly of ancient leather shoes and crocodile purses. That, not to mention the present caper, forced me to be all business. "If you are serious about more 'Picassos,'" I said, "I'll need some different paints."

"What the hell? You brought a whole sack of paints."

I explained about drying times. "Goldfarber got me several cans of Johnstones' emulsion that worked really well. They'll still be in his studio."

Harry made a face. "Where they'll stay. Police have it locked up like the crown jewels. But you're not going to do a 'Picasso' in house paint."

"Correction: I've done a 'Picasso' in house paint." When he looked skeptical, I added, "Richard didn't notice, did he?"

Harry thought about that and shrugged. "Richard doesn't know damn all. But I doubt you'll get good house paint in Tetouan. I'll have to go back to Tangier for it."

My idea exactly. "That's fine," I said. "I'm not going anywhere." I made a list for him and saw him out the door with the reminder that time was short. Once he was gone, I went into the kitchen, ate the salad, bread, and wine I'd been left, and prepared to go out. Despite Richard's threats, I planned to find someone willing to take me across the strait or along the coast to Tangier, where I could attempt the ferry as Jerome Hume. The idea of leaving the Zone on legitimate transport, courtesy of Richard's phony papers, was almost irresistible. Indeed, I saw so little wrong with the scheme that as soon as I finished eating, I took the torch and made my way toward the flickering lights of the port. The road was steep and unlit except for the moon. Now high in the cloudy sky, it cast deep shadows under the palm trees and streaked the road black and silver.

I kept alert for feral dogs and loose stones and fellow travelers of one sort or another. Occasionally, I heard a restless donkey or a horse, and near one large house, someone playing a melancholy Arab melody on a flute. Elsewhere, darkness and silence and the pervasive uncertainty of moving half-blind in unfamiliar places: shades of the Blitz and patrolling dark London streets. How swiftly the past returns at some moments. I thought of Nan and Arnold, who'd loved me, better, I feared, than I had loved them. These were bad thoughts, but I knew the cure. I reached a ramshackle cafe near the water and climbed the listing steps to the door.

The low, cramped interior might have belonged to an ancient

merchant ship or some ghastly freighter. Smoke hung like a London pea-souper, barely penetrated by the single lantern on the bar and the faintly glimmering candles on the tables. The clientele all looked to follow the less reputable branches of the maritime trade. They wore tattered shirts and pants, and their lean brown faces were topped with sea caps or battered straw or felt sun gear. They favored long mustaches and scraggly beards, and they smelled of salt, fish, and gasoline. I got a once-over from their shrewd, avaricious eyes.

Smugglers to a man, I guessed, and so much the better, though the heavy, even sinister, atmosphere could only improve with alcohol. I went up to the bar, and good luck kept me from ordering drinks for the house or a bottle of something bubbly, for when I reached into my jacket pocket, I came up empty. No wallet. A bad moment as I tried my other pockets, before I remembered Harry reaching for my passport. He must have palmed the wallet at the same time.

I'd underestimated him. To be in a rough bar with neither money nor beauty is an awkward spot, and I'd have faced an inglorious retreat if I hadn't found some pesetas in my pants pockets. The bartender poured me a glass, and despite my reduced finances, I set out to make myself agreeable to a man I judged to be relatively sharp and relatively sober and possibly interesting in one way or another.

He was thin and rawboned, and his short hair was quite gray. His face was dark from the Mediterranean sun and deeply lined from the sea wind. He carried a whiff of motor oil, and I noticed that his fingers were stained black, suggesting he had a boat with an engine, suggesting that he could do the run to Tangier. When I found he spoke some French, I bought him a drink, and we started talking.

His name was Xavier: another saint, I was surely destined for sanctity. He claimed to be a fisherman. I claimed to be a tourist who painted picturesque scenery. In pursuit of the Spanish Zone's magnificent beaches and charming villages, I fancied a run along the coast—maybe as far as Tangier?

He made an expressive gesture. As a visitor, I wouldn't realize that it would be impossible to travel beyond the boundaries of the Spanish protectorate. But a run up to Ceuta would be attractive, and he quoted me a fancy sum. If I'd had the remnants of Goldfarber's two hundred pounds, I could have been off and away. But without my wallet, I was stuck on dry land—and dry in every sense, for my resources would just about stretch to another round for Xavier and me.

Just the same, I sounded him out on ways to reach Tangier. Or Gibraltar. "There must be people who need to leave fast and unofficially. People with enemies, perhaps?"

He shrugged again. He did not know personally, but he had heard there were possibilities. Strictly for cash in advance. "You understand, señor, that there are many dangers and difficulties. And only at night."

I said that was too bad since the coast was said to be spectacular.

"Alas, señor, politics interfere with the life of man."

I could agree with that. We had another drink and might have become even more confidential if I hadn't been short of money and if the clientele hadn't kept early hours. The smuggling trade clearly cuts into prime drinking time, for most of the mariners had already left before I headed for the exit, inwardly cursing Harry the Light-Fingered. The British secret service couldn't catch Goldfarber and could neither expose nor protect Angleford, but they'd managed to leave me penniless in the Spanish Zone. Her Majesty's subject could have done without that expertise, and I went trudging up the steep road fast enough to get my lungs protesting.

I stopped beside a dense, shadowed garden to catch my capricious breath, which was threatening to depart for good. I stood wheezing and gasping until a dog howled somewhere nearby. The canine tribe is the bane of my existence, distasteful to me and toxic for my asthma. Fearful of meeting one of the feral packs that roam the hinterland, I forced myself uphill.

The light of my torch bobbed ahead of me, spearing into the ragged shadows of the palms and eucalyptus, the figs and fruit trees. My breath was so noisy that I didn't hear the steps until they were quite close. The road had been deserted only moments before, and I turned around quickly. No lights, no torch. I switched off mine and listened.

Silence. Whoever it was had either turned into one of the dark gardens or was standing, like me, waiting. I edged off the road onto the verge, where dusty weeds muffled my footsteps and the shadows of garden wall protected me from the moonlight. Then I walked on as fast as my lungs would let me.

The road was a gray streak to my right. Everything to my left was in shadow. The footsteps kept pace with mine, but though I kept turning around, I only once spotted the two men who emerged briefly from the shadows when the moon picked out their light shirts and trousers before vanishing behind the clouds. I was in darkness again. I put my hand out until I felt the wall next to me and followed it as quickly and quietly as I could. When it turned a corner, I made my way blindly across a narrow lane and picked up another wall on the other side.

I moved in this fashion for perhaps a hundred feet. When I reached the next cross street, I turned the corner and felt my way along. Almost instantly, something dry and brittle hit me in the face. I almost cried out, before I recognized one of the big flowering vines favored in the area. I felt for the trunk and squeezed behind the mass of leaves, dead flowers, and branches.

I had a chance if the moon stayed behind the clouds and if I could keep from coughing and wheezing. I waited. Now I could hear their steps quite clearly. Would they turn down the lane? I could just make out the faint line of the road. Two dark shapes crossed it and moved away. How far would they go? And how far was I from the rented house, which would be almost indistinguishable from its neighbors in the dark?

I waited what seemed like a long time, then extracted myself from the vine, thinking I needed a more secure hiding place. I'd started along the lane when I heard voices, and I shrank against a garden wall. The footsteps became clearer along with voices, low and urgent, as if they knew they'd lost me. I was sure they would begin searching the side streets, but within a moment, their steps faded. It seemed that I'd fooled them.

Or, I thought, once my breathing was returning to normal, maybe they had nothing to do with me at all. Maybe I had let Harry and Richard infect me with their nerves and paranoia, and my supposed danger was no more than two men, tipsy after a night down at the cafes, returning home somewhat uncertainly. That had to be it, and I was rather annoyed with myself for giving way to fear instead of greeting them.

When I was back on the empty road with silence behind me, I had another thought: they were unwilling to exert themselves, because they were well aware of where I'd be; they were confident of success and in no hurry. That was an unpleasant idea. I waited quite some time and listened carefully, but I heard nothing more, and anxious to find the house, I switched on the torch. Aiming it over the walls as I walked, I soon found the building where I was to be, more or less, a prisoner. From being reluctant to see Goldfarber, I was now almost eager to make contact with him. I needed money, and I needed it quickly if I was to get out of the Spanish Zone and out of Morocco.

With this in mind, I was in the studio early the next morning. My mood was irritable. I had several ideas for paintings, which I must put aside to copy Picassos from what I considered one of the master's less admirable periods. And from rather inadequate images, too, for most of the reproductions in the books were black and white. Just the same, the captions of Richard's selections were encouraging: *damaged*; *missing*; *lost*; and my favorite, *presumed destroyed*—the label on a painting formerly in Dresden. It was represented by a rather muddy color reproduction, one of the few in the book, but I judged it a safe choice, unless the master himself should refuse to authenticate it.

That was a possibility too remote for worry. I planned to be well away from phony Picassos and North Africa before any forgery of mine hit the market. Nonetheless, I hesitated. I hate fakes, and after last night, I feared Richard's scheme might be even riskier than I'd imagined. In the interests of delay, I went downstairs for another cup of coffee.

Elena, the housekeeper, had arrived at dawn, and I'd awakened to the sound of her moving about the kitchen. For a moment, I was back in London, back in my old studio with its high ceilings and Millais' fancy Victorian chandelier. With sudden, relieved joy, I thought it was Nan, up early as always to fix breakfast and, being half-blind, to endanger us both with the gas stove.

Then the white coast light through the shutters, unfamiliar birds in the trees, a whiff of the distant sea; Nan was dead and gone except in the back chambers of my mind. Knowing I wouldn't get back to sleep, I dressed hastily and went into the kitchen. Elena was working at the table, kneading some bread. She was small and dark, past middle age but by no means decrepit—one of those sturdy, domestic, bustling women who keep the home fires burning. When I opened the door, she turned and greeted me in Spanish. So much for her being deaf.

I answered in French and added that it looked to be a nice day.

She smiled and agreed. When I asked for some coffee, she lifted a battered pot from the stove and poured me a large cup. Accustomed as I was to the delicious espresso types of Africa, I was surprised by a bitter but familiar taste. For a moment, I suspected that a quirk in the universe had decreed that everything in the protectorate should remind me of London, of Nan, of the past. Then, more rationally, I took a closer look at Elena.

Despite her iron-gray hair and tanned features, I suddenly doubted that she was either Spanish or Moroccan. It was not just the coffee, or the bicycle that I noticed parked near the kitchen door. No, there was something fundamental in her forthright manner that suggested points farther north. "Will you fix me breakfast?" I asked in English, and I was sure she understood, but she didn't reply, just gestured as if eating.

I nodded.

"*Muy bien*," she said and went to the stove.

Harry had lied about her but lied carelessly, confident that I would take no notice of a servant. He didn't know about Nan and London mornings in my old studio. But who was Elena and why was she here? I guessed she was at least part English and that she'd really been hired to keep an eye on me. Well, I was wise to that. Downstairs, I got another cup of the wretched, if reminiscent, coffee, and returned to the studio.

None of my alternatives were good; all required money, and at the moment, my only source of funds was dodgy paintings. After I'd delayed and organized my painting supplies and stared out the window and killed as much time as possible, I gave in and measured out the photo of the lost Dresden painting.

Fortunately, Picasso had used standard canvas sizes, and I had a stretched and primed canvas of the correct proportions. I sat down at the table, squared up the photo, and figured how much I needed to enlarge the image. Then I took a pencil, and using an extra stretcher as a straight edge, lined my canvas. Once the grid was done, I began copying what was in each of the small squares of the photo onto the larger squares of the canvas.

By the time Harry arrived, much out of sorts and without any emulsion, I had the image sketched and the canvas ready to go.

"Like a coloring book," he said. "You just fill 'em in."

Is such a man born offensive or is it something he's cultivated? "Right. Anyone can do it, and you can do without me."

"Touchy," he said.

"So where are the house paints?"

"Richard said no good. Has to be oils. He doesn't need them dry, he said. He needs them authentic."

I shrugged. I'd at least gotten rid of Harry for an evening. "Tell him then I'll need some racks for carrying them. Otherwise they'll be smeared all over."

"Right, another fool's errand. Never mind the drying. How soon can you get one finished?"

"It depends how motivated I am." I was thinking of my wallet, my hundred-plus pounds sterling, my various escape options. But given Harry's level of vigilance and paranoia, it might be better if he didn't know I'd already missed the money. "Probably finish one today except for the fine details. If it dries, finish tomorrow. If not, start the second—if I get another color reproduction. "

I expanded on this until he grew bored. As myself, I always try to be amusing. Not so as Jerome. As Jerome Hume, I found myself quite willing to be tiresome, and I nattered on while trying to think how to get some cash from him.

But Harry never took off his jacket—wisely, I admit—and I wasn't skillful enough to pick his pants pockets. Not that I was going to get much opportunity. After being reluctant to leave the previous night, he now seemed eager to be off to serious snooping and hair-brained schemes in Tangier. "You must try Elena's coffee before you go," I said. "It's the real thing."

He agreed to a quick cup, and we went down to the kitchen. Elena offered some sweet rolls, which, to be fair, were excellent, though the coffee had much the same effect on Harry as it had on me. I made small talk and watched the pair of them. She looked like everyone's favorite auntie, but I was sure she was at least as fishy as Jerome Hume.

If my suspicions were correct, she was a real pro. There wasn't the slightest sign of recognition between the two of them, which was odd in a way, since he had supposedly hired her. As soon as we were served, she busied herself at the stove with preparations for lunch, giving no sign that she understood a word we were saying. I had my doubts just the same.

"Have you any pesetas?" I asked Harry when I saw him to the door. "All I came away with was pocket change and some large pounds. At the very least Elena will need a tip, and I need some local currency to go about with."

"You don't need to go about at all. You'll stay here and finish those damn paintings."

"Did I waste my breath explaining about drying times?"

"Right. But at the moment there is nothing to dry, is there?"

"A few hours this afternoon will do the trick for one of them. But how are we going to flush Goldfarber if I'm kept in solitary? How's he to know I'm here? I need to get out and about and see things and meet people."

"Painting first."

Harry seemed unconcerned about Goldfarber, although supposedly everything was being done to attract him. I might have questioned that, but instead, I said, "Money after one painting is done or I go no further."

Harry indulged in a bit of bluster about this, but I pointed out that I couldn't do more than one anyway until Richard got me more color reproductions. "I want some pesetas as soon as I finish the first one," I said. "You can change some of my pounds if you must, but if I'm on Her Majesty's business and keeping Gibraltar safe from Reds, I really should be on expenses."

Harry gave a little smirk, and I was sure that he was thinking of my purloined wallet. Then he said, "I'll put in for expenses and get you some cash when that painting is done. In the meantime, Francis, stay put. And stay safe."

Was that meant as a threat? I was soon going to find out.

CHAPTER TEN

I worked dutifully the rest of the morning, mixing my colors as close to those in the reproduction as I could. This proved a tricky business. Photo reproductions of paintings are never exact, and matching colors with different brands of oil paints is difficult. However, I persisted. The great man is supposed to have knocked off masterpieces in a single day's work, and I had the advantage of having the complete design before me. By lunchtime, I had blocked in plausible colors for one of Picasso's weeping, and hysterical women.

Poor Dora Maar; despite the many paintings she inspired, her affair with the great man does not seem to have been a happy one. I can't say I cared for the results, but maybe it was just a case of material hitting too close to home, unhappy loves, and bad, obsessive behavior being much on my mind at the time.

Close to one o'clock, Elena appeared to tell me lunch was *listo*. She asked whether she should keep the food *caliente*.

I held up my hand for five minutes and started to clean my brushes. Was I wrong or had she taken a good look at the painting? *Watch the paranoia, Francis.* Downstairs, I had grilled sardines and a salad with red onions and oranges. Barring the coffee, Elena was an excellent cook, and I told her so in both French and English.

She smiled and nodded, the very model of the modern domestic—complete with a spy camera or a listening device in her capacious black purse? I did notice that she was never without it. When she went into the garden to get some rosemary, I got up from the table and sidled over to have a look. No camera. No mysterious recording device. What I saw instead was a small but heavy handgun. Right.

I got back to my seat and tried to look unconcerned, but when, a few minutes later, she bid me *adios*, I hurried up to the roof. I watched her wheel her bicycle out of the yard and set off down the road toward the port. She turned at the second cross street, where the tall trees in the neighboring gardens blocked my view. Dinner being late in the Spanish style, she wouldn't be back for hours. As for the gardener, I had not seen him yet, and a glance into the yard below told me that he was not on the premises. Just as well; I never fancy being under observation, especially when I'm eager to fly the coop, literally or metaphorically.

But first, I dutifully checked the paint on the newest "Picasso" and convinced myself that it was too damp to add the details. That was good, because I had a serious need for diversion. Despite my new and pious name, the monastic life is not for me, and while cafes and restaurants were out of the question, life is full of possibilities if you have savoir faire. I decided that Jerome Hume had plenty.

He only needed some materials, and fortunately, Richard and Harry had done a thorough packing job; it took but a few minutes to find a pocket sketchbook and some pencils. Although I usually use a brush and do only rudimentary drawings for my paintings, I developed a certain skill at sketching during a brief stint as a beach portrait artist. Now I was Jerome Hume, tourist and amateur landscape painter, and where better to find some local color—and maybe some excitement—than a seaport?

Sketching material in hand, I set off down the same narrow road I had taken in darkness the night before. The mysterious walls and dark gardens were now ordinary enclosures of fig and citrus trees, and the jagged and inky shadows the shade of date palms. I quickly passed the little streets I had managed so slowly the night before and crossed an open field where sheep and goats were grazing, accompanied by some active little boys in short djellabas. The Mediterranean lay ahead, bordered by a dazzling white beach and swept by a brisk wind.

I walked onto the sand. A line of men, some on the shore and some in the surf, were hauling in a long fishing net to the accompaniment of dozens of screaming gulls. The fishermen were thin and muscular; their faces, shadowed by their straw hats, were the color of old bronze. Would Jerome Hume be interested in them? I put down a few lines on paper, but healthy exercise in the open air is not the most congenial subject for me. Still, I had to admit that the coast was spectacular with the sea receding in bands of jade, aqua, and ultramarine until it met the paler stripe of the horizon and lowering clouds to the north.

The port was to my left, a tumble of blocky houses that descended the hill to the docks. A variety of fishing boats rode the water, along with other, sleeker, if no better painted, craft that I guessed handled the smuggling trade. I noticed several substantial yachts, too—early arriving winter visitors or travelers set to cruise to Egypt along the African coast. Although not fond of beaches with their blowing sand and stink of salt and seaweed, I could fancy a yacht.

Unfortunately, I was in an awkward situation: too poor for the virile young fishermen and too old for the rich yachtsmen; life can be a melancholy business. Perhaps that's why Jerome Hume preferred landscapes, poor man. I balanced on one of the pilings that lined the edge of the dock and scribbled in the masts of the fishing boats with their complicated lines and ropes. I added little figures for the fishermen, busy with their catch, and for their nocturnal counterparts, who were sleeping the afternoon away on the decks of slim, fast boats and getting ready for mysterious runs to the International Zone and points farther north.

Some of the locals had interesting faces—bony, weathered, and secretive—but I had no chance to sketch them, for they were as wary as cats. I would no sooner put down a preliminary oval or the line of a jaw before their dark eyes would open, and Jerome would find it prudent to move on to another motif. Altogether, it seemed best to focus on the yachts. I selected a handsome blue sailboat with white trim and a neat little rowboat as a tender. The shape of the smaller boat against the dark hull of the larger ship was interesting—or at least as interesting as inanimate subjects get for me—and I was working on the rippling reflections when a voice behind me said, "Jolly nice schooner, right?"

I turned to see a florid man in a navy blazer and white slacks. Despite his smart dress, I pegged him for a genuine seafaring man, for he was burned from wind and sun, and the thinning hair above a pair of large red ears had been bleached white. He wore a large and complicated watch, no doubt for some nautical purpose, and his feet were bare, all the better, I guessed, for making his way up the mainsail or across slippery decks.

"Very handsome," I said. "But I know nothing about ships. Jerome Hume. Landscape painter." I shook his hand.

"Tony Coates. You've come to the right place, old chap. The African coast is spectacular in every way." He waved his hand toward the white buildings rising from the sea toward the mountains as if he'd invented the view personally and was eager to profit from his creation.

"Indeed, I hope to see more of it."

"Rent a boat," he said. "A cruise along the Med's the thing. Or out through the straits and down along the Atlantic coast. You can't go wrong with Moroccan scenery."

"My idea exactly."

"I'd offer to put *The Aurora* at your disposal, but I've a serious undertaking at the moment. A mission of mercy, so to speak."

"This is your ship, then?"

"It is, indeed. Sleeps six with three in crew. I cruise for pleasure, mostly, but now and again needs must, you know. A boat produces a lot of calls on the old purse. Like to look her over?"

"I'm afraid I'm not in position at the moment," I began, but Tony waved off my hesitation.

"You never know when you'll come into funds, do you?"

That was certainly true.

"And a man of your profession—well, travel is an investment, is it not?" He walked around the end of the dock and stepped onto the deck. I followed, thinking not so much of the six bunks and the mod cons but of nautical hospitality in the form of a nice rum and tonic or a concoction with gin. In pursuit of a drink, I was willing to admire the fine paneling, the compact galley, the ingenious storage, the gleaming brightwork.

We were about to adjourn "topside," as Tony put it, for a "snifter," when one of the bedroom doors swung open. A pink nightgown, a sun hat, a pair of high black heels: there was a woman in residence. Fine, I have no prejudices about women at sea. What was not fine was the drift of newspapers on the bed, all from Tangier and all seemingly open to stories about Jonathan Angleford's death. Was yours truly part of the case, or as I sometimes suspected, had Richard and Harry sold me a bill of goods? I itched to flip through the papers, and I was about to remark that I'd missed getting the English-language news from the Zone, when Tony pulled the door shut with a snap.

Up on deck, we sat with drinks in our hands and the sun at our backs. The brandy was excellent, the sky clear, the sea blue, but I suddenly found Jerome Hume a very thin disguise. If Tony's mystery woman should prove to be Edith Angleford, I'd be in an awkward spot. Although such bad luck was unlikely, I thought that Tony also seemed a trifle uneasy, as if he'd been putting together one thing or another. Perhaps it was just the sight of my sketchpad in conjunction with the stories about the Goldfarber gallery, but he had turned taciturn after being unnecessarily informative about *The Aurora*. The silence became so long that in desperation I asked about his crew.

"Pick 'em up for the return trip," he said. "There's almost always chaps looking for a berth. Strictly short-term, you know. I can't afford to carry a permanent crew, more's the pity. But, like now, we may be here a couple days, maybe a couple weeks. Fool's errand, if you ask me. But when the old exchequer is empty . . ."

His voice trailed off, and he looked so depressed that I asked what his "mission of mercy" involved.

"A woman," he said with a sigh. "A woman bent on vengeance like—what's her name? Medea, was it? You wouldn't believe it now, old chap, but I was a Greek scholar at Eton."

He was right; I didn't believe it. Maybe he'd just spent too many years before the mast, but on closer acquaintance I thought there was something rum about him. His accent wasn't quite right and his "yachting outfit" suggested a touch of fancy dress. I wondered if the handsome schooner was really his or if he was just a crewman with pretensions. Not my concern either way. What I wanted to know, and half-feared to learn, was the identity of his current employer. "There were a lot of vengeful Greeks," I said. "There'd be no classical literature without them."

"You are so right."

"And you've got yourself a Greek?"

"English as you and me," he said dolefully. "But bound and determined, just the same."

"She'll put you in a dicey spot if she succeeds—accessory before the fact, possibly; accessory after the fact, certainly. You could face a myriad of unpleasant legal possibilities."

"The curse of the law. Being short of funds is a terrible thing, putting a man into difficulties not of his own choosing."

I could certainly agree. "Do you know who her target is?" I tried to speak casually and to avoid looking nervously down the dock.

"Target uncertain. She wanted one and then she wanted another, and now I think she's after them both."

"And this is because of—"

"Didn't I say, old chap? Her husband, of course. A writer fellow up in Tangier who was murdered by some pansy gallery owner and one of his painters. A bad lot all the way around."

"A disgrace to the profession," I said with a fair show of indignation. "But they've left the International Zone, have they?"

"Well, that's the interesting thing," he said. "Edith—no last names now, you understand."

"Perfectly." To be honest, I needed no more. A writer murdered by a gallery owner had to be Jonathan Angleford. And Edith had to be his dearly beloved, who was already angry with me.

"Edith got a heads-up from someone fairly high in the ranks. Seems one or both fled to the Spanish Zone."

"A wide area." I must hope that she was set to canvas the entire protectorate.

"The gallery owner is well known here," Tony said. "I understand that he runs some sort of smuggling sideline. He'll show up here sooner or later."

"And the painter?" I asked cautiously.

"Forger, we should say. Oh, he'll be holed up somewhere nearby. He's dependent on the gallery owner for sales, don't you know."

I sure did. With this dismal fact in mind, I lingered only long enough for another brandy and the information that Tony's "Medea"—really, he could never have been a Greek scholar anywhere—had gone to Tetouan for the day. I wanted to be gone before she returned, although every time I made a move to leave, Tony pressed me to stay. The sun, as he put it, hadn't yet "dropped over the yardarm," and when it did, we could leave off casual afternoon drinking and get down to some serious consumption.

Music to my ears, normally, but Jerome was of sterner stuff. He had sketches; he had inspiration; he had canvases awaiting. Once off the yacht, I walked up through the town, because I was not entirely sure Tony was as obtuse as he was pretending to be, before doubling back to the beach road and the track into the hills to my street. I listened at the front door and checked the house cautiously but it was empty, although someone—Harry, Richard, Elena, the invisible gardener—had left me two new books on Picasso that included color images of paintings inspired by Dora Maar. I had no more excuses and must get back to work.

For the rest of the week, I fell into my London habit of painting from early morning until well into the afternoon, a routine made easier by the fact that I wanted at all cost to avoid Mrs. Angleford. Even after Harry came through with a little walking-around money, I stayed away from the picturesque docks and confined my visits to a couple of cafes too seedy to attract a woman like Edith. My habit was to drink until the sun began to set, returning just before dark and well before Elena arrived to fix a late dinner around nine p.m. I devoted the rest of the evening to studying Picasso reproductions, with the thought that the sooner I got the paintings done, the sooner I'd be free of secret service types and crooked art dealers.

As a result, within a week I had four medium-sized canvases complete, two more bone-period biomorphs and a couple of weeping Dora Maar's. If I did say so myself, they were pretty damn convincing, and although I'd hidden my initials in each of them, I was confident they'd pass muster. Certainly they'd be good enough for Goldfarber's nouveau riche clients. Harry was impressed, and I could have packed up my brushes but for one little detail: we hadn't seen or heard from Goldfarber.

I was alarmed by his silence. A long vacation on the Moroccan shore was not on my agenda. Harry was completely unconcerned, lecturing me on the patience required for clandestine activity. I thought our activities seemed more like garden-variety fraud and brought up my missing pounds sterling as part of the argument.

"All in due time," he said, although he parted with a nice little roll of pesetas, which enabled me to spend a riotous afternoon with Diego, a young smuggler, who was such a charming fellow that I decided I could get fond of onboard frolics. We had a parting drink at one of the nicer cafes, and I lingered afterward, feeling for the first time since I'd been shanghaied by Her Majesty's minions, like a free man. The sea breeze was freshening, the gulls were crying, and

I was finishing a glass of Spanish white in excellent humor when I became aware of a shadow cast by someone too close to my chair.

"Jerome Hume! Fancy seeing you again."

I recognized the almost posh accent with something a little off about the vowels: Tony Coates, Mariner to Medea. I was prepared to be cordial, to hoist a few glasses at my own expense, but he sat down abruptly and added, "Or should I say Francis Bacon?"

Well! Cards-on-the-table time. "What do you want, Tony?"

"I see you don't deny it. Took me a while, old chap, to work it out, but the press photos don't lie."

"It's a put-up deal from start to finish. I never met poor Angleford. Not alive, that is."

"You would say that, though, wouldn't you?" Tony turned and signaled for the waiter. He'd have a Fundador, a double, on his friend's tab. I guess that was me. I waited. Tony waited. His drink arrived. He said it was satisfactory. I said I was pleased.

He drank a good deal of it, as if his system had needed topping up. Then he said, "I have a proposition for you."

This was obvious.

"I'm embarrassed for funds. Hence Medea. I've been promised a bonus if I can put her in the way of the man who killed her husband."

"That would be Goldfarber."

Tony nodded. "She would like him, but the papers have been very clear that a certain painter, Francis Bacon, is involved. Killer or accomplice or accessory or some such. I'm not up on all the lawyer lingo, old chap."

"There's maybe something to be said for suttee," I observed.

Tony gave a barking laugh. "Indeed. One widow less would suit me fine, but I can't afford to lose her, even if you seem like a decent chap."

I acknowledged that decency only gets you so far.

"My problem is money," he said. "I don't really care how I get it, so long as I get *The Aurora* free and clear. Personalities have nothing to do with it."

"That certainly reassures me, Tony. But what do you want? Check my wallet if you like. I don't have more than a few pesetas to my name."

He waved his hands. "If you had money, you'd be out of here," he said.

"Better tell Medea I'm in the area and collect your bonus."

He nodded his head, rather sadly I thought. "I may be forced to do that, but I'd rather not. A bird in the hand, true, but I'm thinking further down the road."

I can't stand a man who mixes metaphors. "To the point, Tony."

"Well," he said, with a sly look, "I'm thinking you might be more profitable long-term than Medea."

Tony was a bit slow on the uptake, but that didn't mean he was not dangerous. "How so?"

"You're a painter. You were working with Goldfarber. I've put two and two together."

"I'm a painter; he ran a gallery. There's not much you can make out of that."

"I've been checking up," Tony said. "He didn't carry any Bacons. He carried Picassos and Manets and other expensive Frenchies." He leaned closer across the cafe table. "I need a painting—a good, expensive one."

"And what do I get out of it?"

"I keep Medea off your tail. And you get someone who can fence forgeries. Forget Goldfarber. I can get paintings into Spain, France, and England, because *The Aurora*'s fit for sea voyages. I take the work off your hands, and I pay you a steady income. No more dealing with queer foreign homicides, eh?"

"I don't have any paintings," I said.

"That's a lie and that's stupid. If we're going to be partners . . ."

"And if we're not?"

"I stand up now and call for the police. I'll do it, old chap."

I downed the dregs of my wine and thought it over. He *would* do it, I decided. He was just stupid enough. Then, besides having Edith Angleford after my blood, I'd be in trouble with both the Spanish police and Her Majesty's representatives. I stood up. "All right," I said. "One painting. Where should I send it?"

He gave me the sly glance again. "I'll come collect it now," he said.

CHAPTER ELEVEN

The quick Mediterranean night descended as we walked up from the beach. The sky had clouded over; the rising moon was only a fitful presence, and in the darkness various ideas about eliminating my companion drifted through my mind. I should have acquired unarmed combat skills or a handy stiletto; without these, I resorted to playing on Tony's nerves. I mentioned the rough, deserted ground where sheep and goats grazed by day and the many shadowed gardens, byways, and side streets. "I'm not usually out this late," I said. "Not since I was followed by a pair of toughs my first night."

Tony grunted noncommittally.

"You may not want to walk so far carrying anything valuable. We can wait until tomorrow if you're at all nervous . . ."

"I've got the cure for nerves," Tony said and patted his jacket.

"Entirely up to you," I said. "There's a bit of everything in this neighborhood." As if on cue, a donkey started braying nearby. Tony jumped and put his hand under his jacket. I had hoped he was packing some liquid courage, but he was yet another devotee of firearms.

"Tomorrow, you could be back in the Zone," Tony said.

"If only I could. I've told you, I'm flat broke."

"Yet you are living very nicely. Maybe I should look into that."

I thought to myself that he would not like what he'd find, but I said nothing, and we made our way to the road and then to the house. Still all dark. I fumbled for the key to the gate and felt Tony's pistol against my right kidney. "Nice and easy," he said.

"My thought exactly."

I opened the gate, locked it again behind us, then unlocked the house. I felt for the candle that stood on the table nearby and struck a match. "Wait here," I said. "I'll get you a painting."

"No chance of that, old chap. You might have anything upstairs."

I hesitated, then shrugged. Whether or not he saw that I had other paintings scarcely mattered. If he could sell one, he'd be back for more.

We went up the narrow stairs. The candle cast a pale circle of light across the floor, across the ceiling, across the easel with Dora Maar in cubist hysterics, and over the finished canvases facing the wall. I went to pick one up, and it was only when I turned around, painting in hand, that I saw a movement in the shadows, a figure with one arm raised. The candle jumped with the shock, but before I could speak, a nasty thunk jounced my heart, my liver, and most of my other internal organs, as Tony dropped to the floor like a poleaxed steer. Casually professional, his assailant stepped into the light and picked up the pistol that had rattled onto the tiles. Herr Goldfarber looked no more congenial than when I'd seen him last.

I thought it prudent to set down the painting and raise my hands. He patted my jacket and pants pockets. Then, satisfied that I was unarmed, he put away the pistol and lit a cigarette.

"Let's see the work," he said, as if we were back in the fancy gallery and I was a hopeful painter with pictures to sell.

I turned the canvases.

"Portraits of Dora Maar. I don't know if they'll do quite as well. There's maybe a bit too much angst in them for the Mediterranean world." I heard disgust in his voice, as if there was something reprehensible about a taste for light and happiness.

"The originals are presumed destroyed," I said. "Safer by far. Make up provenances and you can sell them anywhere."

"I see you have been thinking ahead."

"I've been forced to, thanks to you. Why did you kill poor Angleford?"

The dealer laid his heavy hand on my neck, a gesture that definitely did not connote affection. "That needn't concern you."

"Of course it concerns me. I've been blamed for it."

"A piece of luck for me," Goldfarber admitted. "But what happened to my painting?"

"A long story. Too long for now, but there are four 'Picassos' here. Well, three available. I've agreed to trade one to Tony there for his silence."

"Tony will be silent in any case," Goldfarber said in a heavy tone. "Pick up the paintings and let's go."

When I hesitated, he gestured with Tony's pistol.

"They are all damp," I said. "That's genuine oil paint. Nothing but the best for you this time. We'll have to put them in the racks, and you'll have to carry at least one if you don't want them damaged."

He really had an inventive German vocabulary, but he waited until I put the three finished paintings into carrying racks, leaving the final Dora Maar on the easel. I took one painting in each hand. Goldfarber took the third and followed me out to the street. "Take a right," he said.

I saw a large dark car parked in the shadows. Goldfarber opened the boot, and I loaded the pictures. I had faint hopes of the gardener, my perhaps mythical protection, or of a miraculous recovery by Tony, or of some other providential alteration in the universe.

"Hurry it up," said Goldfarber.

"You want them damaged?"

"I'll see to them myself," he said and shoved me aside.

I should have taken off immediately, but I was still weighing my chances and getting up my courage when I heard the distant squeak and rattle of a bicycle: Elena coming to make dinner? Very probably.

"You really need some proper packing," I said in a loud voice. "Something to separate the canvases. With all the bumps on these roads, you'll have a problem for sure."

Goldfarber was not keen on advice. He slammed down the lid of the boot and gestured for me to get into the car.

A beat in which I felt my heart and heard my breath but not the bicycle. Either I'd been mistaken or Elena had heeded the warning.

"I'll only be a problem. You know I'm wanted for murder," I said and edged away from the car. Goldfarber was remarkably quick for a large and bulky man, and he caught my shoulder. I hacked him in the ribs as hard as I could, but though he was surprised and staggered, he did not let go.

I believe that Jerome Hume would have been in for some serious damage if a female voice had not cried, "Stop right there!" in perfect English. I'd been right about Elena.

"He's armed!" I shouted, and things fell apart in that moment, for a shot pinged off the open car door.

"It's Jerome," I called, "don't shoot!"

She didn't, but Goldfarber fired blindly into the darkness, and in response, several more shots landed in our neighborhood. Clearly

Jerome Hume was expendable. I dropped into a crouch, aiming to make a run for it, but Goldfarber grabbed me from behind and shoved me into the car. I tumbled into the passenger seat, where I struggled to get the side door open. But before I could find the handle, Goldfarber's shots were answered with two that shattered the windshield, covering me with shards of glass and sending me into the well of the dashboard. He fired once more before he slammed the car into gear, and we careened forward.

More shots against the doors, against the hood, a final rattling against the back fender, then we were lurching and bouncing up the road, weaving from side to side in the darkness and threatening every wall and tree until Goldfarber finally switched on the remaining headlight.

I'd figured that he'd make for the port, the smuggler's base, and our potential exit from the protectorate, but we turned inland, with the windshield a spiderweb of broken glass, the engine roaring, something a bit dodgy with the back end, and only a single wobbly light to show us the way.

While Goldfarber was occupied with steering the powerful car up the dark, narrow road, I found the door handle and prepared to dive onto the tarmac. I told myself that we couldn't be going so very fast, although with the breeze coming straight in over the dashboard and the rear of the car listing alarmingly, I had more than the usual sense of forward motion. There was also Goldfarber to consider. If he'd killed Tony—and he might have—he'd want to leave no witnesses.

So have you an exit strategy, Francis? Not really. I'd blown the money I had on my afternoon with Diego, who ran cigarettes into the Zone, and my painting equipment was back in the laughably unsafe safe house where Harry had stashed me. Would Her Majesty's minions trust me if I went back? Could I get back? I was still mulling my options when Goldfarber screamed, "Hang on," hit the brakes and nearly overturned the big car with a high-speed U-turn.

He had seen something ahead, and now I did too: car lights and an impromptu barrier. Our single headlight bounced over the dark faces and handsome uniforms of the local gendarmerie. Goldfarber could not quite manage the turn, forcing him to back up, change the gears, wrench the wheel. I kept my head down as shouts were followed by a rattle of fire from the barrier. A jolt as Goldfarber hit the brake, then a lurch as he floored the accelerator. The big car shot away, back toward the port. When I thought we were out of range, I looked out the rear window. Through a mesh of cracks and splinters, I saw twin headlights down the road.

"They're following us."

"They won't catch us. German engineering is still the best in the world." He did something fancy with the steering wheel that enabled us to miss a palm tree close to the winding road.

"Speed won't do us much good if you put the car into a wall or hit a stray donkey."

"You want to take your chances with the Spanish police? They'd like a murder suspect better than a traffic offender any day."

He'd no sooner spoken than he hit the brakes, sending me into the dashboard with a thump. I grabbed the door handle just the same, and I would have risked the tender mercies of the protectorate police if Goldfarber hadn't precipitously turned the big car into a narrow lane, where he switched off the light and gunned the motor. Vines slapped along the sides of the car and branches rattled off the roof. We dropped down a steep and bumpy hill before he risked putting on the light, which bounced off bushes and fences and the occasional farmhouse wall.

When he turned again onto a slightly better road, I saw the flat silver of the Mediterranean; we were headed for the water. I had a brief hope of finding friends at the port before we entered such a maze of little streets that I soon lost all sense of direction. Goldfarber clearly knew the area well, and except for the bullet holes and some damage to one fender, the big car was intact when we finally pulled up to a tall gate. He stopped the car, drew the pistol, and gestured for me to get out.

"Open the gate," he said, and handed me a key, large and heavy enough to have opened a dungeon. "If you run, I'll kill you."

He was certainly a man who made his intentions clear. I opened the gate and stood to one side, but he waved me back into the car so that I had no chance to slip away. He had me get out and open a garage door next. It was only after the car had been safely stowed and the gate relocked that I got a look at the remarkable house. It was made of stone, the local boulders I guessed, and it had a lumpy, handmade look at odds with its enormous size. It was on three levels, and on two of those were terraces with built-in planters, all filled with cacti and other spiny plants. The overall effect was of some huge fetish, but whether it was designed to produce good or bad luck I could not tell.

Goldfarber motioned me forward, unlocked a carved wooden door, and shoved me into a two-story entrance hall that smelled strongly of paint. *Oh ho, Francis.* Could this be the "private house" where the late "Spanish boy" had labored? Goldfarber found a lantern with a candle and lit it. Someone was planning a Moorish design on the white plaster walls, because an enlarged arabesque had been traced in a band perhaps eight feet off the floor.

"Very nice," I said. "And when did you promise to have this finished?"

He gave me a sour look. "The Spanish police will comb the area, but they will take no notice of a workman. I have a smock for you and a cap. Trust me, you'll be invisible."

"I doubt a smock and a cap will hide that car."

Dexterous as a lizard, he slid his arm around my throat. "Do not concern yourself with anything but the project at hand," he said.

I was strongly tempted to bring up my predecessor, whose labors had been so violently interrupted, but it did not seem to be the moment. Goldfarber gestured toward the stairs, and I soon found myself in a small room, with toilet en suite and ornamental ironwork on the small windows.

"Breakfast at seven," he announced before he went out, locking the door behind him and leaving me with only the cloudy night sky for light. When my eyes adjusted, I tested the window grills, but they were all strong and well fastened, and this time Goldfarber had not made the mistake of leaving a key in the lock. I appeared to have traded down from HRH's custody to that of a homicidal crook, forger, and spy.

"Sleep on it, Francis," my old Nan used to say. That seemed like not just the best, but the only plan at the moment. I lay down on the narrow bed, pursued by fractured images of dark roads and blinding lights and by painful, if half-formed, anxieties about David and about yours truly's chances of returning to the Zone. The next morning, the key rattled in the lock just at seven, before a good-looking young Moroccan came in wearing a spotless white djellaba and a crimson fez, a pleasing start to any morning. He gestured for me to accompany him downstairs, but disappointingly, my breakfast was to be solitary. The Moroccan appeared again to clear the dishes and a third time with a blue workman's smock and a soft cap. I put them on and followed him into the hallway.

In daylight, I could see that while the design was attractive, the execution was sloppy at best, with the colors inconsistently mixed and crudely applied. Either Goldfarber had gotten a bad run of help or the project was simply an excuse to hide "workmen" of one sort or another. For what little good it did me, I strongly suspected the latter.

I examined the paints—mediocre oils in rather unpromising shades—while sizing up the Moroccan servant. Could I cast my charms in that direction? Could my pitiful few pesetas buy me an exit? Should I part with my watch, my last negotiable item? I smiled at him and gave him a wink, but his dark face remained immobile and severe. Perhaps he was pious. Perhaps he was political. Perhaps he believed in whatever scheme Goldfarber and his masters were running.

The possibilities made my head ache, and I turned with a certain amount of relief to the work at hand, mixing up a particular shade of turquoise and filling in a sharp-pointed repeated motif. It was mindless, meditative painting once I had the right color, and I worked my way across the room on the scaffolding. Goldfarber was nowhere in sight.

But the local police were. They arrived midmorning, after I had finished the turquoise and moved on to a deep cobalt that gave poor coverage and was going to require numerous coats to cover the elongated diamonds of the design. The Moroccan opened the door and greeted the cops in an animated mixture of Spanish and Berber. From what little I could understand, the *patrón* was away, the repair and decoration work was behind time, and there was no one in residence but himself and the *pintor*—a gesture toward me.

They wanted my papers, nonetheless. I climbed down and handed over my documents, half-hoping they'd arrest me and half-anxious that they might. As it turned out, two of the three were illiterate, and their superior clearly read with difficulty. He matched my face to my photo, and after satisfying himself that I spoke almost no Spanish, handed back the passport. "*Bueno*," he said, but I thought he gave a significant look to my Moroccan keeper.

A moment later, they adjourned to the back for what I expected was some convivial food and drink. The local force seemed familiar with the house, and I suspected that they were paid off not to look into its affairs too closely. I returned to the scaffold in a thoughtful mood. I now doubted that the police would be any use at all. Getting out of the house would probably be doable, as the Moroccan had to sleep at some point, but I needed cash to get clear of the protectorate.

Then, I had an interesting idea—the Muse does sometimes whisper the completely unexpected. I'd been assessing my prospects all wrong. I didn't need cash if I could only get to the port. Edith Angleford wanted Goldfarber, and I had found his base. I hoped that fact and my well-known charm would be enough to secure Mrs. Angleford's approval and my ticket out.

I certainly needed the latter, because with four paintings in his possession, Goldfarber not only had no more need of me, he might even see me as a liability. Enough noise from the British consulate could still push the protectorate police into action, and that would complicate whatever rackets Goldfarber had going at the moment. As I began adding a burnt-orange octagon to the centers of the basic motif, I realized that I needed an exit soonest.

That afternoon, I told the Moroccan that I needed a break. The hallway was not well ventilated, and with the paint fumes and a little effort I managed to start wheezing. You can bet I played that up. His face remained stoically immobile, but after I really did stagger getting off the scaffold, he held up his hand and disappeared into the back. He returned almost immediately with the addition of a large and lethal-looking knife in an ornate scabbard.

His weapon produced an all-too-vivid image of the dead "Spanish boy," my predecessor. I might have been wrong about Goldfarber, who was all blunt instruments and brute force: a thump on the head or manual strangulation seemed to be his MO. His Moroccan employee, on the other hand, was maybe the hand behind the knife.

When he gestured toward the door, I was so loath to turn my back on him that I moved sideways toward the exit. This amused him considerably. He made a brusque gesture, strode to the door, and unlocked it without another glance as if I presented no threat at all. Annoying, but I had no time for vanity. To be underestimated might turn out to be an advantage, and I certainly had few other resources at the moment.

We stepped into the brilliant North African light and walked along a white gravel path to the garden, which in its own way was quite splendid, being full of spiny, twisted shapes, at once fleshy and thorny. Picasso must have known similar gardens, and I might have been inspired, too, if I hadn't been checking the high wall and the locked gate. We did two circuits of the garden, at the end of which I had narrowed my possibilities to a lone palm tree that grew at an angle toward the wall. Though I detest exercise, I've always climbed very well. *Onward and upward, Francis!*

The pleasing idea that if I could leave the house, I could escape the garden got me through the rest of the afternoon. Of course, there were less pleasing thoughts, like speculations about Goldfarber's return, the destination of my "Picassos," and the possibility that the Moroccan was tipped to be my executioner. I did my best to ignore them.

Around six o'clock, the servant returned to signal that I was done for the day. He'd produced a respectable goat stew and a salad with oranges and the inevitable mint tea. I was just finishing when I heard heavy steps in the hall. Goldfarber came into the kitchen and sat down. The Moroccan brought him a plate of food, and he looked at it for some time in silence. The gallery owner often created an oppressive atmosphere, but this time I detected something different. He seemed less angry and more depressed, as if some plan had turned out other than expected.

Perhaps I was right, because he sighed, and without touching his meal, lit a cigarette. "You do nice work," he said after a moment.

"Another two days maximum—well, maybe three. That cobalt blue pigment is very cheap and thin."

Goldfarber grunted. "Pity you won't get to finish it. Decorators are hard to come by."

I thought that he should be more careful with his artisans, but I didn't say anything.

"You've done enough so that I can finish up myself." He drew in the smoke, exhaled, and watched the plume ascend to the ceiling.

"You've done decorative painting?"

"I've turned my hand to a lot of things," he said in a reflective tone. "Few of them congenial. But the war . . ." He made a vague gesture.

"Needs must," I said, and I was reminded of Tony. I wondered if he was recovering from a bad headache or if he was even now gathering flies in some protectorate morgue.

"You in the West have no idea," Goldfarber said. "The possibilities for disaster were infinite and the possibilities for survival miniscule."

"Yet here you are."

"Yes, and I intend to survive, even with regrets. Some—even some of the best—chose otherwise. Not me."

He leaned forward and fixed me with his stony eyes. If nothing else, he was an unusually forceful and energetic personality. I could believe that he would survive at all costs, and I expected that nothing good for me was going to come from this extraordinary prologue. He leaned back again and took another drag on the cigarette. "I genuinely love art," he said after a moment. "In another, better life, I'd be running a gallery, strictly legit, and you'd be happy to have me handle your work."

I thought that it would have to be a very different life, and I'd have to be a very different painter. Still, I appreciated that there might be more to Goldfarber than a temper with muscle. "And in this imperfect life?" I asked.

But Goldfarber was lost in reminiscence or fantasy. "I packed paintings," he said. "That was one of my jobs. And appraised artwork. There was a lot floating around."

"Stolen?" I asked.

"Appropriated. The Nazis had a taste for euphemism. And no, I'm not German."

"Not Jewish, either."

"Few people know that," he said complacently. "I've found a flexible identity a great asset. But Samuel Goldfarber is not going to be around much longer, thanks to your admirable work. The 'Picassos' need only a signature, and I am doubtless more adept at that than you are. A few sales and I can start over, perhaps in South America. I think I could fancy Argentina." He tapped the ash off his cigarette. "So I am grateful to you, Herr Bacon. Very grateful. I want you to know that. I would genuinely regret it if you thought otherwise. And that has put me in an awkward position regarding your future."

I didn't like the sound of that one bit. I almost preferred the brutal and exciting side of Herr Goldfarber to this glimpse of something reflective but still sinister underneath.

"You present a problem for me." When he tipped his head to one side, I felt I was being assessed by some large and indifferent carnivore.

"Nothing like the problem you've presented for me. Even if I walk out of here tonight, I am still entangled in a murder case in the Zone."

Goldfarber shook his head regretfully. "Not enough trouble, unfortunately. But I have a solution for both of us. I wash my hands of you, and you will, in all probability, never hear about the Angleford case again."

"What have you in mind?"

"Not in mind, in motion: I am turning you over to the Soviets as a British spy.

CHAPTER TWELVE

I took a moment to digest this bizarre idea. "You can't be serious. You know I'm not a British agent. Never was, never could be. I'd be considered a security risk guarding a slit trench never mind the secrets of the realm."

"You'd be surprised," Goldfarber said. "You really would. But just as you are, you'll do fine. You are traveling under fake documents." He reached into his pocket and pulled out my Jerome Hume passport. That mix of desert asceticism and Scottish rationalism had never been a good idea. Goldfarber opened it with ostentatious care and read off the name. "We both know you are a painter named Francis Bacon."

I couldn't disagree with that.

"And you have been living in a British safe house, guarded— not too efficiently, I must say—by the British agents who are hot on the trail of whoever killed Jonathan Angleford. The KGB will know all of this already," Goldfarber said. "They will be prepared to believe that you are deeply involved. By the time they decide you are of no importance—and thanks to the inertia of the Slavic mind, that will be quite some time—Samuel Goldfarber will long have ceased to exist."

"I'll tell them that you're sick of Reds and dealing forgeries." I was embarrassed at how feeble and schoolboyish that sounded—*please sir, he's been smoking in the WC*—and yet it was the absolute truth.

"Of course you will," Goldfarber said. "And you will deny being a British spy and all the rest of it. But you see, they will *know* different. They will have made up their minds."

"They'll still suspect you."

"They suspect everyone, and given their methods, they usually confirm the worst." Goldfarber assumed an expression of distaste. "I truly regret this for you. In a better world, all would be different."

"In a better world, would we all be good?" I asked.

"Ah, Herr Bacon, I see you are a philosopher as well as an artist. This is why I feel bad. Were there any other way, believe me, I would take it. But there is not, and my imperative is survival. In this world, that is the only commandment." He stood up and called for the Moroccan in Berber. The man appeared behind me, and before I could react, he slipped a pair of handcuffs on my wrists.

"They will be here soon," Goldfarber told me. "Ayoub will hand you over. This is *auf wiedersehen*, Herr Bacon. We will not meet again."

"Don't count on that!" I dredged up a few choice German phrases from my misspent, if enlightening, youth, but Goldfarber slammed out the heavy front door. A moment later we heard the car start up and not more than a quarter of an hour later—a quarter of an hour in which various fantasies of escape and retaliation were quashed by the Moroccan's impassive face and impressive dagger—another vehicle crunched over the gravel drive and stopped.

Ayoub led me into the hallway. He unlocked the door. Two men stepped in and stood shoulder to shoulder like Tweedledee and Tweedledum. Both were cut from the same pattern, short and wide shouldered. They had bad haircuts and worse suits. Their broad, Slavic faces were marked by weather and age and hard living, and their eyes were fathomless. These were the men that Goldfarber had feared, and it struck me that I should be frightened, too.

They said nothing, but the older of the two motioned with his head. Ayoub seized my arm and hauled me outside to a large black car. I braced my feet and said, "This is ridiculous. You are kidnapping a British national. My consulate—" but I didn't get any further, because either Tweedledum or Tweedledee gave me a tremendous blow to the right kidney. I dropped with a gasp onto the gravel, only to be jerked upright by the handcuffs and thrust into the backseat—so much for the power of the empire.

The older man got in on my right side. His companion walked around and slid in on my left, the seat of the car sinking under his weight. The doors slammed shut. The driver, thinner and darker with a narrow mustache and a long scar across his forehead, put the car in gear and hit the gas, spraying stones right and left as we passed through the gate and out onto the road.

I leaned back against the seat and struggled to catch my breath without disturbing the sharp pain radiating across my lower back and exploding with every bump and pothole. When my heart rate dropped, I risked a glance at first one and then the other of my companions. They stank of tobacco and unwashed shirts and some strong, low-quality alcohol. Both sat staring straight ahead, looking tough and remorseless.

I seemed to be descending the abduction ladder, with captors of greater viciousness on every rung. This was more than my usual sort of pickle, and I struggled to focus on how I should act and what I should tell them—and when, too, because I had the feeling that I would soon be talking more than I'd ever intended.

We left the port road and headed toward Tetouan, raising brief hopes of a traffic slowdown and a lucky escape. But no, our route lay toward the mountains, where the moon rising over the Rif touched the ridges, leaving the stony slopes deep in shadow. Our car lights picked out woods and fields and the dark tents of the occasional Berber encampment, and I felt my heart sink: the countryside never brings me luck.

Not this time, either. The car pulled up at a stout and isolated building with a couple of decayed sheds and some crumbling fencing. One window had the faint golden glow of an oil lamp; no other lights were visible. We were a long, long way from anywhere, and another look at my companions suggested that not much civilization could be expected. They dragged me out of the car and into the house, which smelled of damp and old fodder and domestic animals. I started to sneeze the moment we stepped over the threshold.

The driver, whose name was Kirill, lit another lamp. We were in a sort of dining room/dormitory, with three camp beds arranged along the back wall and, in the center of the room, a large table holding papers, a short-wave radio, and several bottles of vodka. Chairs doubling as a resting place for a variety of garments were arranged around the table; there were no other furnishings. This was strictly a place for work, and I didn't like to dwell on what that work might be.

Two doors opened off the room. One, I guessed, would lead to a kitchen. The other, I soon discovered, was a cell, pitch-black after the lamplight. I was frozen until I located the wall nearest the door, where I stood, back against the bricks, waiting for my eyes to adjust. The only light came from a sliver seeping under the door and a tiny square of moonlight from a barred window near the roofline.

After several minutes, I could take note of my surroundings. My new lodging came with both a bucket latrine and a water bucket—backcountry mod cons—what proved to be a straw mattress on the floor, and an immensely heavy straight chair whose arms, I realized with a shock, were fitted with leather straps. Nan spoke in my ear plain as day, "You're in for a bad time, Francis."

How right she was. But first my captors had a meal. I smelled the now familiar Moroccan spices and heard shouted commands in bad Arabic. They had a servant, maybe more than one. The agents themselves talked back and forth during the meal, but quietly. Of course, I was right next door, and I was supposed to be a British counterintelligence agent who would know Russian and all the tricks of their trade.

If I could convince them of my ignorance, they might see that they'd been fooled. I'd have to be very clear about my role and very willing to be helpful. Yes, I thought that best. I didn't owe either Richard or Harry heroics or stiff upper lip stuff. Besides, I had no secrets to reveal. None whatsoever.

I sat down on the mattress, which was every bit as thin, rough, and dubious as I expected, but I wanted nothing to do with the chair with its echoes of dentistry and electrocution. I knew that they were going to hurt me, and all too soon, the door opened and the two Russians appeared with an oil lamp. The older one motioned toward me, and his companion grabbed my handcuffs, jerked me to my feet, and transferred me to the chair with practiced efficiency. I was clearly not the first to share their accommodations.

"I am Colonel Lev Yegonov," said the older man. He did not introduce his junior, who I deduced must be the one they called Aleksey and who busied himself undoing my handcuffs and fastening the leather straps in their place.

When all was in order, he went into the front room and returned with a chair for his boss. The colonel turned it around and sat down with his forearms resting comfortably on the back and took a long drag of his cigarette. He stared at me for some minutes, during which time his shadowed features were deeply imprinted on my mind. His large face, looming against the dark wall of the cell, might have slipped from one of my canvases, and I had an odd sense that some of my art had been premonition.

"You are a member of MI6, operating out of Tangier," he said.

"I am a British painter with no connection to MI6."

The colonel made the slightest motion with his head, and Aleksey struck me in the face. Not a slap, but a real blow that sent my head back against the chair.

"Do not waste my time," said the colonel. "Who is your control?"

"I was asked to contact—" I was not allowed to finish before Aleksey hit me again. This is how we progressed. I was torn. I owed Richard and Harry nothing; at the same time, I refused to be coerced. And for someone who lies as easily as I do, it was exasperating to be asked to lie at a moment when the truth might save me. I'd lost a tooth and was spitting up blood before I muttered, "Richard Alleyn."

The colonel leaned back in his chair and studied me. He seemed to be a connoisseur of pain if not of veracity. "Richard Alleyn is a rich socialite in the Zone."

"And I am a painter from London."

I expected to be hit again, but the colonel seemed to be taking this idea under advisement. I was unprepared when he suddenly leaned forward and stamped the red tip of his cigarette against my forearm. "Do not joke with me," he said.

"Working undercover," I gasped. "Has been since the war." A nasty smell of burned meat hung in the air. The colonel drew on his cigarette and exhaled a cloud of smoke. I felt my lungs seize up. There is something to the "straw that breaks the camel's back" theory. Amid the mildew, straw, old animal hair, and the smoky oil lamp, the colonel's vile tobacco was that last straw. I began to cough and then gasp. Aleksey hit me twice, but my lungs put me beyond their reach. I needed air so desperately that even my present circumstances counted for nothing. My brain screaming for oxygen, I strained against the straps, attempting to inflate my chest and suck in more air.

My condition must have alarmed them, because Aleksey undid the straps. By then I was semiconscious. He moved me over to the mattress, and when that proved ineffective, he picked me up and carried me with a shout to the other room. Kirill opened the door and let the clean night air flood in. That and a little vodka helped, but we had no more questions that night.

In the morning, I had recovered enough for another session in the chair. It did not go much better. I should have listened to Goldfarber and dropped what I now realized was too high a regard for truth. But though I gave them Harry at the consulate—the only detail that fit their preconceptions—and attempted to describe Goldfarber's forgery racket, they were not content. They wanted some elaborate plot. They wanted me to be someone important shipped in from London, and deadly serious men themselves, they didn't like the idea of anyone as seemingly frivolous as Richard. I really think they found him an offense to their profession.

I was in serious shape by afternoon. My whole body throbbed, my face was bruised, my eyes were swollen nearly shut, and blood from my lost teeth had sickened me. I had burns on my arms and, worst of all, I was in terror of another severe asthma attack. In the back of my mind, I suspected that I might never leave the cell alive.

I wondered what David would think of my disappearance. Would he ever connect my defection to his legal troubles? Would he miss me? You can see that I was in a bad, defeated way, and if Nan had not kept whispering in my ear, "Think, Francis," I might have put my head down and tried to blot out everything. She wouldn't let me.

Of course, I was thinking about how David was getting on and not about clever plans to escape the colonel and convert disaster into triumph. That was too much to expect under the circumstances, but thoughts of David led me to happy memories of wild nights in Tangier, which, doubtless because of my injuries, led me to remember the night we'd discovered Nadir, the supposed revolutionary, lying beaten in the street. Even that might have gone nowhere if the Moroccan servant, young and soft-footed, had not come in just then with a glass of mint tea and a little bowl of couscous.

When his dark face bent over me, I remembered the night and day in my studio and the injured man and his gift. I held up my hand for the Moroccan to wait, then I struggled to sit up so I could search the pockets of my slacks. Nothing—they were empty, every one, and I felt despair rising to meet me before I touched something round, metallic, almost forgotten: the embossed bead from Nadir's strange bracelet. I handed it to the Moroccan. "Nadir," I said, and I saw his face change, taking on a new, keen, determined look, before I fell back onto the mattress. That was my last, best shot. He would help me or he would not; Nadir's name was powerful or it was not. I could do no more.

CHAPTER THIRTEEN

Although I didn't realize it at the time, my asthma attacks must have frightened the colonel, because they threatened the loss of a prize already promised to Moscow. As Goldfarber had been frightened of them, so the colonel and his men were frightened of certain mysterious Soviet powers, who communicated their wishes via the whistling and buzzing radio. These powers did not like to be disappointed, and they had their own ways of dealing with failure.

As a result, I was given a reprieve, with no more sessions in the chair, although that sinister device was left in my cell as a reminder. I also got three meals of soft food a day, very welcome given my sore mouth, and little glasses of vodka that turned toothless sockets to fire but kept infection at bay. When the combination of ancient dust and new smoke started my wheezing, I was even allowed spells outside. All this counted as luxury; truly, everything is relative.

A day passed . . . two, three. I regained my strength only to realize how hopeless my position was, for I could see no way to escape three professional and well-armed agents. As for the Moroccan servant, my ray of hope amid despair, he gave no sign of having passed on my message. He did not smuggle a knife to me. He did not appear in the middle of the night to escort me to safety nor arrive at the head of a troupe of Berber warriors to effect my rescue.

One casts one's bread upon the waters, says the proverb, but sometimes the loaf sinks. Nadir's bead, however well meant, did not bring help, and on the fourth evening when the colonel entered my cell with Kirill and Aleksey, I knew it was too late. Kirill grabbed my arms, still sore with healing burns, and Aleksey pulled up the sleeve of my shirt. The colonel handed him a hypodermic needle.

I kicked and struggled and bit Kirill's hand at one point, but they were too practiced for an amateur. I felt a sting like a bee, a fullness in my upper arm, and then, rapidly, for though I have a great capacity for alcohol I am often sensitive to drugs, a cold drowsiness flooded my senses. I saw the cell, and their faces with their brutal features and matter-of-fact expressions. I saw the chair, the buckets, the walls, the lamp, and suddenly the notion of going to either Moscow or the moon was a matter of indifference.

What happened next is just random images and conjecture. Surely I was dragged out to the car. I saw the ceilings in the house and the night sky overhead, blossomed with stars. Darkness and lost time, before a wave of nausea raised me, choking and retching, from the druggy depths to spatter the seats with vomit. A sudden halt. Shouting, angry voices. The colonel moved up to the front seat, and I was left beside Aleksey, who sat cursing the mess.

More darkness. I was sailing on a choppy sea. I was whirled on a merry-go-round. I was drunk without being disorderly and floating in the night air. Then with a jolt, I was flung against the front seat and realized that I was in a car. In a car in Morocco with KGB men who had a fantastical scheme to peddle me to Moscow as a British agent. I was dreaming and it was all unreal, until I heard the car doors opening, the colonel's shouted curses and directions, and Kirill's answering profanity. The car seat heaved as Aleksey got out, and I raised my head.

I must have vomited some of the drug, for I was suddenly aware of the dark Moroccan night, noisy with insects, and of the narrow road blocked. By rocks? Were those rocks? Yes, tumbled, I thought, from the steep hillside to our left. The road was too narrow, the drop on the right too dangerous for Kirill to attempt to drive around. Now Aleksey had gone to help him, because the boulders were enormous, and the colonel, impatient, had stepped out, revolver in hand—oh, wasn't he a cautious bastard—to see if a stream of Russian curses would move the work along.

I felt for the door, for the handle, my head pounding and my breath rushing in and out like a steam train. Could I do it? The colonel was only a yard away. Too close. But he was going to inspect the boulders. I was sure that it would take three of them to roll one, and they would have to put down their weapons. They would.

I pressed the handle. A thunderous click, which amazingly they did not notice. The door, now, the door. But first legs, did I have legs? I actually had to put my hand down and touch my knees. Legs. Move. Slowly. Push the door. Move the legs. Find feet. Find ground. Hard to do with head somewhere high above earth. Out.

A sound, a new sound, behind me. Not the colonel. Not Aleksey. Not Kirill. A new sound, a new shape, a new person that touched me and breathed one word in my ear, "*Silencio*," before several shots shattered the car lights that had illuminated the road, the boulders, the sweating KGB men and left us in darkness with our ears ringing.

"*Vamos*," said a voice in my ear, before I was dragged across the road and down a steep slope covered with shrubs and rocks. Such a descent really requires legs and feet, and I seemed to have either one or the other but not both. I could feel rocks and gullies and crackling branches; I could feel my knees moving, making an effort, but feet and legs refused to connect.

One shot, then another came from the road. Someone pushed my head down, and unbalanced, I tumbled, small stones finding every one of my bruises and scrapes, until my precipitous descent was stopped by a thorny bush. Hands pulled me out. I was aware of flashes and bangs from the road and of dark figures and of the night sky chilly and full of stars. Nothing more.

There was light. Not starlight, not car lights, but the genuine item, daylight, glittering white through the holes in a black fabric. I was lying on the ground on a rug, and I smelled disgusting. But stink is real, and this was no dream. I was somewhere in a tent minus the handcuffs and the chair with the leather straps.

I sat up. I had legs, feet, arms, hands, torso. I also had a monster headache and a sour stomach. But still. I stood up. So far, so good, though I could see now that my jacket and shirt were stained with vomit, blood, and dirt. I staggered to the door of the tent and looked out as a donkey ambled by. Horses were tethered a dozen yards away, and I saw some camels, too. This was country living with a vengeance, but for once I was thankful.

A woman with a tanned face and gold earrings saw me, and I waved. She disappeared instantly, and I sat down in front of the tent to wait. Presently, a tall, slender man with a patriarchal beard, heavy, graying brows, and an alert, intelligent face appeared. He had the thin, well-defined features of his tribe and one blind eye, blue-white with cataract, which suggested he was older than his straight back and quick stride suggested. I found the locals' ages difficult to estimate. Their hard lives aged them prematurely, while their dark skin concealed some of the damage.

"I am Issam," he said. "How do you feel?" His French was heavily accented but comprehensible.

"Relieved," I said. "And grateful and very dirty and sore."

He nodded. I looked at his lined and worn face and suspected that our concepts of hardship were quite different. "Nadir said that he owed you his life."

"Please tell him that he has all my gratitude." It occurred to me that his had been a difficult decision if indeed his group had been getting money from the Soviets. "He might have survived in Tangier without me, but I would never have survived in Moscow. Never."

Issam agreed with this. "They are ruthless men, so we must get you away as soon as possible. Can you walk?"

"Oh, yes. I was drugged last night, but I am all right now."

"You must eat. Then we must get you to the port and back to the Zone."

This was a delightful program but difficult to accomplish. For one thing, I had only a handful of pesetas, although Issam agreed that my fine gold watch should be acceptable to a smuggler.

"We, of course, need no gifts or money," he said with great dignity. "To help a friend is a duty, *inshallah*. The boatmen are a different matter." He frowned as if acknowledging that the good old ways had been eroded by commerce.

"They take risks, so they deserve to be paid," I said, although I would regret the loss of the watch. I detest men who wear jewelry, but a real gold watch is a useful signal that one has the means to treat the young, the poor, and the beautiful. On the other hand, having recently contemplated eternity, knowing the exact time now meant a little less to me.

There was also the problem of eluding the Soviets, who were

bound to be furious and on the alert for any sign of yours truly. That was why, coached by Issam and to his great amusement, I rode into the port on an extremely wide and uncomfortable camel. I was swathed in white wool like a Berber out of the backcountry, barefoot with my telltale shoes in a bundle on my back and with a scarf hiding my light hair and European features. We arrived at the fonduk toward dusk in a big company of traders and their beasts, and even the primitive accommodations were a welcome sight after two days in the saddle. We spent the night, hidden in plain sight, and I remained there the next day, nursing my sunburned legs beside a surly camel, while Issam negotiated my passage to the Zone.

At last he returned with the news that I would leave shortly after midnight. "It will be dangerous," he said. "The Russians are in the port, the colonel and his driver."

"And Aleksey?"

Issam shrugged. "He is perhaps in the town proper in case you try to go overland. They must not know that you leave by boat, as they have the means to follow you."

I did not like the sound of that at all. Have I mentioned that in addition to disliking the beach I hate trusting myself to wind and waves?

"But they do not know the port as we do," Issam continued. He explained that I would have a guide—a local man, a fisherman—who would take me to the smuggler and return with my borrowed clothing. I counted out the last of my pesetas, and Issam said that they would have to do. I suspected that Issam and his friends would now owe some favor to the fisherman, and I felt a little guilty at the risks that these brave, poor men had run for me.

Issam just waved his hand and told me to sleep the rest of the day.

The moon had risen and set before he returned again with the small, dark figure of the fisherman, who signaled, without a word, for me to follow him. I embraced Issam and whispered my thanks, then slipped out of the fonduk behind my guide, my shoes chaffing my burned feet, and my legs and back still aching from the unfamiliar exercise on the camel.

Strings of lights lit the medina, but we kept to the dark side streets as much as possible, leaving me to stumble behind the fisherman or rather behind his battered straw hat, which was often the only thing visible in the darkness. We reached the beach and walked along the hard sand near the water's edge until we drew near the docks, our aim being to hide in the shadows from anyone alert along the wharfs.

We were amid some pilings, when the fisherman motioned for me to take off the scarf and the djellaba. I handed them to him, and he made up a bundle and slung it over his shoulder. I had to take off my shoes, too, as we waded through the weedy shallows under first one and then another dock. I could hear the water slapping against the pilings and sucking against the shore. Somewhere, a motorboat started up, and I heard the soft splash of a paddle. The fisherman stopped to listen. He had not said a word since we left the fonduk, but I could tell now that he was nervous, that something was not right.

I stood beside him, listening, and I heard the smoother purr of a more modern and powerful engine than the rackety motors of the locals. I looked at my guide, whose face was brown and wrinkled like an old apple. I could not read his eyes, but he saw my expression and nodded. "*Ruso*," he said.

Of course they would have a boat, just as they had a short-wave and a powerful car and a chair with leather straps.

We waited calf-deep in the water for what seemed like hours. Finally, the fisherman touched my arm and moved confidently out from the pier and along to a listing and decayed wharf. A narrow boat was tied up at the very end in the deeper water. It was lit by a small oil lamp, and I saw that there was a man in it, who, by the looks of things, was sorting out some problem with his engine. Small wonder, for the boat looked to be in alarming condition, and it was already riding low in the water. I was to be supercargo to some mysterious and heavy shipment. The fisherman nodded and pointed to a ladder up the far side of the wharf, then he turned and slipped away.

I waded forward, passed under the structure, and climbed up the ladder. I had almost reached the top when I heard footsteps. Not the barefoot slap or the soft-sandaled steps of the locals, but the sharp sound of hard-soled European shoes. I pulled my head back.

The steps went to the end of the wharf and stopped. Could I get back down? Back under the pier? Out of sight? Footsteps again. I was only a few yards from the smuggler's boat, but to reach it, I would have to cross the top of the pier and clamber down the other side. Why hadn't I let Arnold teach me to swim? I could be gliding underwater to emerge seal-like beside the boat. Instead, I was clinging to a wet and weedy ladder, and some marine organism or stray pollen was tickling the back of my throat, so that without warning, I sneezed.

Steps above. I dropped down into the water with a splash. I tried to run, but the water was up to my knees, and I was floundering toward the shore when I heard the colonel's voice. "Stop, or I will shoot," he said. "Put your hands up and turn around."

I did as I was told. He was a darker shape against the night sky, but some distant light glistened off the barrel of the revolver.

"Mr. Hume," he said. "We have been looking for you." He gestured with the gun. "Up, come back up."

I sloshed through the water, wondering if I dared hide beneath the pier, but no. There were gaps between the boards, and the colonel had come right to the edge. He would have a clear shot, and I had no doubt that he would take it.

I climbed up the ladder and stepped out onto the deck of the pier. My heart was pounding. How dreadful to have come so close to safety only to be caught at the last minute. I stood with my hands up. Down at an angle, I could see my would-be smuggler, still fiddling with his engine. Was there still a chance? Or would he now light out with his regular cargo and leave me to my own devices?

The colonel motioned for me to step away from the ladder. Looking at it from my point of view, there was a certain humor in his caution. He really had convinced himself that I was a dangerous agent, a man of lethal skills and secret trade craft. Now he pivoted, leaving a good space between us.

"Empty your pockets," he said.

I turned them inside-out to show him I had nothing.

"The shoes," he said, impatiently. "The shoes."

I'd tied the laces together and slung them over my shoulder to keep them dry. I held them up and turned them upside down, losing my socks in the process. The colonel seemed almost disappointed.

"Walk," he said and gestured toward the shore.

This was it. I was going to be back in the hands of the KGB. Back in the cell, back in the chair, back, I supposed at some point, in the car on my way to a little airstrip. I stood still; I'd had enough.

"Move," he said.

I didn't budge.

The colonel raised his revolver. I saw the glint of light along the barrel and then heard a sort of pop. I'm dead, I thought, I'm dead because I feel nothing but the night wind. And then the colonel came unstrung like a marionette with its strings cut and dropped to the boards. Someone was running toward the pier and calling, "Jerome! Jerome! It's Harry."

Oh, no! I ran to the far side. My smuggler was sitting in the boat's stern, looking alarmed. I gestured for him to help me, and I scrambled down the rope ladder he'd strung to the side of the pier. I got one foot into the craft, which slid away under me, before he grabbed my arm and pulled me on board.

"*Vamos!*" I said to him. "*Rapido! Rapido!*"

He started the engine, as Harry appeared at the edge of the pier. "Jerome! Come back! You're safe now."

"Fuck off, Harry."

I stepped into the bilge water and sat down with a thump as the motor caught and the boat wheeled away from the pier and the shore. UK or KBG, I'd seen enough agents to do me a lifetime.

CHAPTER FOURTEEN

It took two nights to reach Tangier, with an uncomfortable day laid up in a little cove near the border. As we waited for dark, my smuggler fiddled with the engine, a roaring beast noisy enough, I'd have thought, to wake the entire Zone at any hour. Yours truly lay in the shadows of the rocks desperate to avoid more sunburn. We pushed off when the moon went down, and we reached a little creek east of the port in the misty dawn. I shook hands with my taciturn companion, bid farewell to my gold watch, now on his wrist, and, stiff and footsore, began the trek to the medina.

The sun was up, and I was staggering by the time I reached David's rented house. I pounded on the door until he threw open an upstairs shutter to let loose a stream of profanity.

"It's Francis!" I shouted. "I need help."

The door opened a few seconds later. David stood there in his

bathrobe, looking disheveled and hung over. "For Christ sake," he said
when he saw me. "What's happened? Where the hell have you been?"

I took a step forward and collapsed in his arms. "You won't
believe me," I said.

And for a while, he didn't. It was only when I was lying in the
bath with my many purple and yellow bruises, raw burns, and peeling flesh on display that he sat down heavily on the toilet seat and
said, "Good Lord!"

He brought me brandy and went out for food and was, in
every way, very kind. Not perhaps David in his most exciting
mode, but a welcome incarnation at the time. He wrapped me up
in a sheet and said, "Rest," and I did. It was not until early evening, up, shaved, clean, bandaged, and dressed in proper clothes
that I broached my plans.

"I need you to be very military," I said.

His expression turned serious. Of course, he was half-drunk; I
was sure that he'd been sipping whiskey all day. At the same time,
David could function with an amazing level of alcohol. "Right," he
said, perceptibly straightening his back. "Are we facing Messer-
schmitts or Junkers?"

"Much worse. Top brass."

"I see."

I explained what I hoped to do. "You'll need to be a hero and
pull rank."

David looked skeptical.

"Do you have a better idea? The KGB thinks I'm a spy; the police
here are convinced I'm a murderer, and your friend Mrs. Angleford
is armed and bent on revenge."

"It might work," he allowed. "Two years ago it would certainly
have worked. I'd have pulled it off." His tone was bitter. "Now, I'm
not so sure."

I patted his shoulder but found nothing to say. He was a brave, twisted man, half-ruined by the war and busy completing the destruction. But I could not afford to dwell on that. "Tonight," I said, "because I must get out of the Zone. The only question is do we meet him early or late?"

Early meant people were sober, and things could be accomplished. Late meant people were drunk and might be amenable. Finally, David, who knew the drinking habits of most of the Zone expats, said, "He always changes for dinner."

"Always?"

"Without fail. We will catch him at home around ten p.m."

In the cab up the Mountain, David looked very white and serious. He had unearthed his old RAF uniform, complete with decorations. "A little warm for this climate," he remarked, "but clothes make the man."

I found the sight at once impressive and painful, knowing only too well the gap that had opened between the smart, brave pilot he'd been and the wreckage seeking oblivion in Tangier. But Goldfarber was right: survival requires a certain ruthlessness. I found I had plenty, and I hoped that David still had enough.

We left the cab a block before Richard's house and walked to his walled garden. While I hid in the shadows of an aggressively leafy plant, David rang the bell. The gray, stooped butler, equally renowned for his tact and his memory, appeared. He told David that he was very sorry, but it was too late to see Mr. Richard, who would be going out shortly.

David put on his "voice of command" and said, "Official business. Tell Richard that we must have a quarter of an hour of his time."

The butler shuffled away. We waited some minutes, so perhaps Richard was indeed dressing for dinner. Then more lights went on, and he appeared at the door, looking spiffy enough for the Court of St. James.

"David!" he said in a tone that reflected both the hour and the uniform. "This is a surprise."

"And I have another one," David said, as I emerged from the shadows. "Francis has returned."

Richard was clearly taken aback, but he automatically attempted finesse. "I hadn't realized his absence. The busy social season, don't you know." He attempted to shut the door, but David already had his foot inside, and I slipped in after him.

"We need to talk," I said. "We have things to settle."

For a moment Richard's face was a study, dismay and anger fighting with his usual bonhomie. Then he led the way to a small study, dark with glossy blue Moorish tiling and equipped with a large desk and some filing cabinets. There were more telephones than even the complex social life of the Zone could possibly require, as well as big topographic maps of Morocco.

"Sit down," he said. He studied me for a minute. "Of course, your capture by the Soviets was most unfortunate."

"I was on my way to the Lubyanka," I said. "That was beyond 'unfortunate.'"

"Yes, yes. Quite," Richard said, although his expression, which I'd always thought genial, had subtly morphed into indifferent. "Though everything possible was done. And you gave us quite a lot of trouble. You know that you had only to put yourself into Harry's care the other night. You'd been assured you were under our protection."

"Like Samuel Johnson's patron's, your help arrived after I had other assistance."

"We'd be most interested in learning about that," Richard said with his first show of real interest. "Help from the native community can be invaluable and would go a long way to clearing your copybook."

David had been sitting looking pale and distant. Now his expression changed. He had been on the aerial front line, while Richard and his ilk plotted in underground bunkers, and I knew that he liked nothing better than to call the brass to account. "Francis has no need to confide anything, and he certainly hasn't blotted his copybook, as you phrase it.

"Let me put it to you, and I speak now officially. You and your agency have, for your own reasons, one, falsely accused a British subject of murder. Two, involved an untrained and unsuitable civilian in an agency operation. Three, incompetently designed and run said operation, in the process, deceiving a civilian about his situation. The upshot was, four, that you exposed him to manifold dangers, including torture at the hands of KGB operatives. Is that about right so far?"

"Francis was already assisting the police," Richard began, but David cut him off.

"At your connivance. I don't know what you threatened him with, although in the last few hours I've begun to suspect whatever it was involved me. Which has made me angry and when I am angry, I am reckless. Do remember that, Richard."

He said nothing.

"Now, here is the situation. Francis has been accused of murder. It must be made clear immediately and publicly, without any hedging or conditions, that he had nothing to do with Angleford's killing.

"The KGB has been convinced that Francis, under the name *Jerome Hume*, is a dangerous MI6 agent. The fact that one of their agents was shot during his escape lends credence to that theory. Francis needs his own passport back, and he needs immediate transport to England."

"After a little debriefing, maybe," Richard said. "It would be helpful to know what the colonel was after."

"Finally," David said, ignoring the interruption, "there is a little matter of two hundred pounds sterling taken by one of your associates to prevent Francis from leaving the protectorate, a theft that puts paid to any assertion that he acquiesced in this bizarre scheme."

Richard had gotten very red in the face. I suspected that my entanglement with the KGB meant less than the ungentlemanly accusation of theft. "You realize that I can have you both detained under the Official Secrets Act."

"No," David said, "that won't work. Just try arresting a gifted and popular painter and a hero of the Battle of Britain and see the reaction. My friends in the Forces have been apprised of the situation, and unless you help us tonight in the way I've proposed, you will be finished socially in Tangier. And that will end both your cover and your usefulness to the agency."

Richard attempted indignation. "You would jeopardize your country's interests over a few pounds and a few bruises?" He began to witter on about the importance of the "Moroccan Mission" and the whole Cold War geopolitical situation, but I spoke up.

"Letters have been written," I said. The letters, to be sent in case of my death or disappearance, were actually to a variety of my press contacts, but it didn't hurt Richard to imagine that they were bound for RAF brass and Whitehall chiefs. "And don't think of getting them; they're in safe hands." They were, in fact, deposited with the postal service and winging their way to my dealer in London.

Richard took some time to accept the situation, so long that he'd missed dinner altogether before there was a meeting of the minds. David and I pledged our eternal silence on everything to do with the "operation" in the protectorate, and Richard, though still with very bad grace, ordered his driver to take us all to the consulate. There, a little glue restored my image to my proper passport, and a trip to the safe produced two hundred pounds, somewhat more than Harry had actually lifted, but I considered I'd earned the bonus.

"A flight is next," David said.

"Surely Francis can take the ferry to Gibraltar." Richard was as offended as if his butler had demanded the Bentley to run errands in the medina.

"With KGB agents on the lookout? Direct flight to London's the ticket."

More discussion, followed by phone calls. Eventually, diplomatic pressure produced a seat on the next direct flight to London.

"I suppose you'll want a car and driver, too," Richard said sarcastically.

David nodded. "And fix it with the police commissioner. We don't want any delays at the airport."

More phone calls. It was now well after midnight, and various functionaries had to be called from their beds or, more likely, roused from the pleasure palaces of the town. Finally, the arrangements were complete, a remarkable demonstration of bureaucratic wheels in motion. Richard poured us each a brandy and sat studying me with a malevolent expression. "What did the Soviets want?" he asked.

"Oh, this and that. Mostly who my control was."

"And you said?"

"I gave them you, but they didn't believe me."

Richard raised his eyebrows. "A most unfortunate admission in any case."

"It was under duress. And then I gave them Harry, but they will know all about him now anyway."

"Yes. He might well have spared the colonel just at that moment. Harry's usefulness is compromised now."

"I'd have been compromised if he hadn't," I said.

"And just how did you get to the port?"

I shook my head and stood up. Brave men had helped me, and I had no intention of betraying them to Richard, whose only thought would be to turn them to account. "Sorry, I never involve friends and acquaintances," I said and turned toward the door, staggering on my sore feet. David took my arm.

"Have your driver take us home, Richard," he said, and he led me confidently to the hall and down the marble steps. In the car, we exchanged satisfied glances, but we remained mute as long as we were in the custody of Richard's driver.

Back in David's house, I hugged him, and we both started to laugh. "We must have champagne. We must be drunk and glorious," I said, although I was sore in every muscle and missing skin all over my pelt.

David endorsed this program. We sat in the kitchen with my last bottle of Chablis—my champagne, unfortunately, was long gone—eating dates and oranges. It was like old times, the good old times, when everything was fun, and David's demons were resting, and I still felt like a boy. "That was simply marvelous," I said. "He believed your influence reaches the skies! You were superb."

"Yes, I was. For the last time, I am sure, but still." He gave a sad smile. "Remember tonight when you think of me."

I hated the valedictory sound of that, though tonight was precisely what I would remember, having seen him at his best and glimpsed my own heart's desire. "Come back with me," I said impulsively. At that moment, forgetting all past, and even recent, history, I wanted nothing more. "I have enough money for your ticket, for ferry and train if not plane. You can be back in London within days."

David stood up to take off his blue-gray RAF jacket. He held it in his hands for a moment, with what thoughts and memories I cannot begin to imagine, before folding it so carefully that I sensed that he was putting away a lot more than just a garment. "It didn't work out before," he said. "Why do you think it would work now?"

"Even if it doesn't, come back. It's not just me; you don't belong here. You do still have friends in the Forces—that much is true. Go back to what you do well. Go back to your own country, to England."

"I'm sorry, Francis, but you're wrong. This is my country now. It has everything I require. Tonight, I returned as far as I can ever go. That was a parting gift for you; look at it that way and forget any other hope."

We took off at dusk over the green water and flew toward the setting sun for several hours. I had a small bag in the overhead compartment and two of my *Owls* and an unfinished *Pope* wrapped up in brown paper in the hold, nothing else. I'd left my Moroccan friend the few blank canvases in my studio. My traveling painting kit was presumably still in the protectorate, but I had art supplies in London, and despite the rigors of the last weeks, I found myself full of ideas. I even believed that I might make the deadline for my next show, if I could just get another advance from my dealer, and in between service from the bar cart—presided over by a very handsome steward—I began composing an appeal to her good graces.

I began with the positives: *The Owl series has gone well, and I am returning with several canvases that I am very pleased with.* Technically, of course, two is not several, but it is understood in appeals for funds that a certain expansiveness is allowed. *I've worked hard on the Pope series, too.*

That was jolly well correct, although I was thankful that my dealer would never see the pile of slashed and recycled canvases. But once in London, the *Pope* in the hold would be finished and the series resumed. The *Popes* were popular sellers, and thanks to the colonel, screaming men had a new and pungent relevance for me. I pondered how to suggest new ideas and inspirations along those lines without giving any specifics.

I was much more eloquent on my other plans. When I got back to my essential Muybridge and the images from *The Human Figure in Motion*, I would *begin some paintings using his photographs of wrestlers. Wonderful, ambiguous images of violence—or sex.* That might alarm her just a little, but I trusted her courage, for censorship and threats of prosecution could only boost sales. *Oh, yes, I have ideas*, I assured her.

Completely true. My affair with David, who was so bad for the actual application of paint on canvas, had proved a wonderful source of inspiration. Yet, as the horizon subtly darkened, I felt not exactly depressed but melancholy. It was over, or as good as over, with David, and having seen him momentarily at his best—brave and smart and generous—that parting was even more painful than I'd expected. He was my great love, at least in the sexual arena. I wondered if a willingness to suffer was the definition of the real thing, or if I was a special case with particular desires. Either way, I doubted that anyone else would conjure the intense emotions that David had.

Then, too, I was aware, in a way I hadn't been before I arrived in Tangier, of my age, of time creeping up. Maybe it was just the bruises and a blossoming set of aches and pains, maybe it was just the murky vision of the world behind my protective dark glasses, but I was no longer young and full of promise. All my earlier lovers had been older, much older. Now I found myself contemplating the trim buttocks of the steward and realizing that now and forever more, *I* would be one of the older men. I hoped that I would be rich enough to enjoy that.

I intend to work very hard this next month, I concluded my letter. *I am confident that I can make the opening.* I wasn't really, but I did intend to work hard. *Tangier was a time of turmoil and trouble, and I suffered a rather nasty auto accident while on a brief trip into the Spanish protectorate. My dear, they had to bring me out on a camel! Even that has proved inspiring, so do send the money to me at my London address.*

That seemed a little bald, but there is really no subtle way to ask for cash, and the flight back had rather strained my finances, because Richard had drawn the line at paying for my plane ticket when, as he put it, I had "money in hand."

I signed, *Yours faithfully, Francis*, and pushed the call button. I asked the handsome steward if I might have an envelope. He said that he would try to find one, and I slipped him a pound. "Have a drink on me when we land."

"If you'll have one with me," he said.

All right, Francis! Here was a gracious lad, a high-altitude treasure, and my heart rose. If I was very much the worse for wear, I was not quite finished yet.

CHAPTER FIFTEEN

I returned to my new studio. It was a drab, modern affair, but after Nan died, there were too many memories in Millais' wonderful old Victorian rooms. His studio had been grand with a crystal chandelier; this one was low and cluttered, the floor filled up with books and papers and scraps of canvas and photos torn from the newspapers. A mess not to everyone's taste, but I was reassured by the papers crackling underfoot like leaves. There were ideas down there, ready for the taking.

Not that I needed much help at the moment. Although sometimes I missed louche Tangier's brilliant light and ravishing colors, I can only really paint in gray and cloudy London, where the whitish sky provides an ideal, even light without much glare. Of course, compared to semitropical North Africa, London was cold and drab. With war damage and bombed-out ruins and the stink of coal dust, it was not a city to encourage false hopes; in short, it was my kind of place, and I got right to work.

More than anything else, painting gives shape to my life. I can do without it for a while, as a drinker can give up alcohol for a spell. I can cavort in Tangier or Monte Carlo or wherever, but sooner or later I need a brush in my hand and a canvas on the easel and an image fit to depict internal weather. The world I see is just raw material, and I usually find what I need in other people's paintings or in artistic, press, or scientific photographs.

I don't copy these; rather, I listen to their suggestions, and when I find the right source, the mental floodgates open. After my return to London, there were days when I could hardly get paint on canvas fast enough. I owed this to David, as well as to Muybridge's photographs. All my adult life, I'd searched for the intensity that I found with him, and my new paintings tried to make sense of him and of Tangier.

By the time my dealer arrived several weeks later, curious about the work and anxious about her investment in the upcoming show, I had a respectable number of canvases finished. The two *Owls* from Tangier, a couple of large *Popes*, and—still on the easels and only half-done—my new work, the paintings of naked wrestlers after Muybridge. One pair of fighters was set in the sort of schematic room I often use. I like to create a space that is not illusionary but symbolic and suggestive like the compressed spaces of dreams.

The other pair was within a similar construction but with a floor of grass, and the bodies of the grappling men, lying one on top of the other in a wrestling move, looked like the shadow-striped bodies of wild animals. I was still painting the grass, a matter of lots of individual strokes in different greens, browns, ochers, and blues with a long, thin, liner brush.

Even though the painting was not quite finished, my dealer stood for a long time studying the wrestling men with her arms folded and her head to one side. She is short and dark with a blunt, square face, strong features, and a businesslike manner. The latter, thankfully, is deceptive. She is a rebel and a romantic and as fond of a gambling flutter as I am. But instead of roulette, she puts her bets on painting talent. Best of luck to her!

"This is very good," my dealer said, unconcerned with (or possibly hoping for) a scandal.

Though I'd known the work was good, I was pleased, because it meant that an advance would be forthcoming. Even a broken heart could not keep me from going out on the town—or, recently, to the airport, where my charming steward sometimes met me on layovers. I liked to treat him to a good dinner, and champagne was becoming increasingly expensive.

Naturally, or maybe, unnaturally, I still wrote to David. I complained about the weather and prices and rationing, which was a way of saying that I missed him. He did not reply. I heard from friends that he was playing the piano nightly at the Meridian and that he'd moved to a smaller house. On bad nights, I thought about David a lot. On those nights, I stayed late in the bars in Soho and walked home down dark and deserted streets not many hours before getting up to paint.

On one of those nights, when my Chablis consumption threatened to overwhelm even my stalwart metabolism, I had the first inkling that something was wrong. I'd left the Europa well after midnight, but when I exited the Tube with the moon up and the Thames running silver, the world was so bright that I thought, *bombers' moon*. Old habits of mind, especially old fears, are hard to shake.

I thought that was why I felt uneasy, that it was a little psychic echo of the Blitz and the rocket attacks. I was, after all, in an area that had been hit hard, and I still remembered the clouds of smoke and fire and ash. Yet, the next day, I remained faintly troubled. There had been no fire in the area, not even a big plume of industrial smoke or steam, which can still sometimes trigger memories of the war.

Sober and busy at my easel, I recalled something else: the sound of footsteps in the otherwise quiet night, footsteps that never quite resolved themselves into a fellow pedestrian, although I remembered looking back several times. Just footsteps. *Was that right, Francis?* Or had there been a shadow, too, sharp in the moonlight and glimpsed for just an instant before it dissolved back into the darkness of buildings or street trees?

In the light of day, night anxieties are supposed to vanish. Instead, I subsequently found myself increasingly uneasy, as I noticed one little oddity after another. Two nights later, someone followed four of us out of the restaurant where we'd met for dinner. I assumed that he was just another patron hurrying off in the rain, but there was a moment when I waved good-bye to my friends, two painters and a photographer, all very merry, and I'd seen—what exactly? A figure standing, as if waiting, in a nearby doorway. He lit a cigarette and discarded the match. Then a cab came, and I was whisked away.

This was an observation scarcely worth noticing, and yet, combined with other little incidents, it strengthened a growing sense that I was under subtle surveillance. Had there not been a few more people than usual wandering by the flat? Men out admiring the river, having a smoke? I now recognized one of them. He was the same short, broad-shouldered man wearing a raincoat and a fedora whom I had seen out on the sidewalk two nights running.

Possibly he lived in the area. Possibly he fought with his wife or his boyfriend and liked to get clear of the house for an hour. Possibly he had griefs and walked for consolation, or had troubles and walked in hopes of inspiration. I didn't think so. The raincoat was ordinary, British-made, and the fedora was a decent one, but his physique—short, broad-shouldered, and powerful—reminded me unpleasantly of the colonel and his associates.

I told myself that surely the Soviets had realized Jerome Hume was a waste of time. In retrospect, I thought that even the colonel must have had some doubts, but he was dead, and who knew what his replacement might think? This led me to another disagreeable thought: what misinformation might Richard have conveyed to the Soviets? He was good at deception, witness all my tribulations as Jerome, and our man with MI6 had been very put out by my reappearance and furious to be bested by two amateurs. Could this be his revenge?

Probably my imagination was running away with me, but if not, I was in a real pickle. After a bad day in the studio when several canvases joined the debris on the floor, I decided to settle the matter. I came home quite early that night. I went to my bedroom, put out the light, and sat down by the window. Sure enough, after an hour, along came fedora-and-raincoat. I saw him clearly as he passed under the streetlight. He stationed himself a dozen yards away under a big plane tree, lit a cigarette, and seemed set to wait.

For me? I was debating whether I should go down and speak to him, when my landlord approached. Martin is blond, handsome, and rich, a charmer whom everyone likes and who has a way of putting people at ease. He noticed fedora-and-raincoat and said, "Good evening." When the man replied, Martin began to chat with him.

I could not make out the gist of the conversation, but I could hear, unmistakably, that the man was a cockney, and I was embarrassed to have imagined a Soviet agent or one of Richard's MI6 pals. "You're not the center of the universe," Nan used to say. *Remember that, Francis!*

Just the same, when I next saw my landlord, I couldn't resist asking him about our neighborhood sentry. "Hasn't he been around nearly every night?"

Martin laughed. "Talked to him the other night! What a character, really quite amusing. He's a private detective of all things, working on a divorce case. He says it's the most boring job in England."

"I should think so around here. Who's married and under seventy?"

Martin's smile shaded into doubt. Then he nodded. "He'll be looking for the correspondent," he said sagely, for he was qualified as a lawyer. "That will be it. As he put it, he was 'sniffing out the love nest'—like something out of the *Daily Mail*. I love it!"

I did, too. I'd been prey to the most ridiculous notions, and when I came back very late the next night and noticed fedora-and-raincoat (did he not have any other clothes?) on the Tube platform, I gave him a wave, which seemed to disconcert him. I felt light-hearted. Tangier and the protectorate and spy services, friendly and unfriendly, were a thing of the past. I was painting with a vengeance and only needed more frequent visits from my friend the steward with the lovely physique to count myself happy. In retrospect, I was already on dangerous ground.

I came down early one afternoon, finished with a good day in the studio and ready for lunch, when Martin called me into the kitchen where he was sitting with *The Times*. "Did you see this, Francis?" he asked and handed me the paper. "I know you're interested in Picasso."

It was an article about an upcoming auction of "Modern Masters," the highlight of the offerings, now on view at Sotheby's, would be two vintage Picassos, including a "very desirable" portrait of Dora Maar and a "1930s 'bone period' image," both from "a private European collection." Right! I would lay good money that they were two of the fakes done by yours truly.

That afternoon, I got myself to Bond Street and went to see the paintings. There was a good variety. A nice little Bonnard—not my sort of painter, but still, bright and handsome; a Soutine portrait that I studied with real interest; and, in pride of place, the two Picassos, beautifully displayed in fine carved and gilded frames. There is nothing like the classic gold frame to set off a painting, and I resolved on the spot never to display my work in anything else.

The Picassos looked smashing, plus, they came with documentation as long as my arm. It appeared that they had gone straight from the master's brush into a "notable Czech collection." They were hidden during the war (hence assumptions that they'd been destroyed) and sold immediately afterward to one Hugo Kovar, the present consigner. I suspected that Hugo Kovar used to go about in the world as Herr Samuel Goldfarber.

Could I prove it? I looked at the paintings with great care. I had, as a sort of insurance, inserted my initials with very small, rough brush strokes in each painting, but now I looked for them in vain. Score one for authenticity, but what were the odds of two "presumed destroyed" paintings turning up immediately after I had painted copies of them?

No, these were my work, but Goldfarber, despite his homicidal habits and vulgar manners, was a pro. He had clearly inspected the paintings carefully enough to find and remove the incriminating initials. It was lucky for me that he hadn't noticed them while I was still close at hand.

Goldfarber had then signed the Picassos very convincingly and used some idle hours to work up their provenances. Those were elaborate and complete; he'd done everything short of a trip to Antibes to have the old man authenticate the canvases.

I'd thought all along that even painted in oils my fakes would be obvious. I had not counted on the ambiance of a big auction house.

The hush. The carpeting. The truly splendid frames. The flattering lighting. And most important of all, the presumption of greatness. I was fascinated, and I looked for so long that one of the staff came over. He was dressed in a gray conservator's smock and wore white gloves—all the better to protect the artwork—and asked me softly (no one spoke even at normal volume in the presence of the paintings) if I had any questions. Although it wasn't perhaps relevant at the moment, his thick black hair, rather rough features, and powerful physique lent him a thuggish charm despite his refined manners. *Stick to the subject, Francis!*

I introduced myself and said that I was a painter. "Studying the technique of the masters is always so valuable," I said.

He agreed.

I asked some questions about the Czech collection and Hugo Kovar but learned little except that he was a wealthy and reclusive art fancier who wished to "further diversify his collection." I'll bet!

"Wonderful work," I said quite sincerely, and I asked what time he got off work. Nan always said, "Stick to Mayfair, Francis," and I thought that Bond Street was close enough. The upshot was that I met him in a pub an hour later for drinks. We got on so well that we went for dinner at my favorite Soho restaurant, which, as usual, was wall to wall with painters, so that Damien Worthing, not long out of Oxford, was impressed. That led to various entertainments of a more private nature, ending with drinks at the Europa Club.

I got back to my flat, satisfied on a number of accounts. I had no doubt at all that Hugo Kovar and Samuel Goldfarber were one and the same. Damien's description was detailed; the erstwhile dealer and former KGB recruit was now a rich, reclusive collector with a weakness for strapping young men like my new friend.

"I'll bet he has a posh house," I remarked at one point.

"Rooms at the Claridge just at the moment," Damien replied.

Nan would have been so pleased: Mayfair was going to be in my future after all. It's an indication of my state of mind, that I was actually considering how best to contact Goldfarber/Kovar when I happened to look toward the end of the street. The lone light picked out fedora-and-raincoat. "Sniffing out a love nest" my foot.

I knew for a fact that no one in the neighborhood kept anything like my hours. No one. The same mental state that had led me to consider meeting up with Goldfarber now led me to start down the street toward the supposed private detective, but though portly, he was quick. He disappeared into the shadows, and I heard a car start up. Perhaps I wouldn't have to look for Goldfarber. Perhaps he had already found me.

CHAPTER SIXTEEN

The next afternoon, I went to the Claridge and asked for Hugo Kovar. Mr. Kovar was not in. I tried calling the hotel that evening, but Mr. Kovar was not answering his phone. I declined to leave a message; he didn't need to know that I was onto him. Not yet.

The Modern Masters auction was set for the following night, and I registered to bid to be sure that I would have access to the main room. I arrived in plenty of time, picked up a numbered paddle, and set a course for the drinks table. There were furs and tuxedoes and some very nice diamonds, but no sign of Goldfarber. Maybe the nervous consigner waited behind the scenes. Maybe the supposed recluse was going to avoid the auction and just collect his check. Maybe he would think to share the wealth with his forger. Or maybe not.

The auction started with some of the smaller paintings, a couple of hundred pounds here, five hundred there. The Soutine portrait

I admired went for little more. I regretted not raising my paddle, but I wouldn't have funds until—and unless—my upcoming show was a success.

On to the bigger name impressionists. A late Renoir, very red and pink. Wholesomeness that exaggerated begins to look like rot. A bigger Bonnard, quite a splendid landscape. With each lot, one or more of the white-gloved staff came out to present the painting, while the auctioneer, very debonair and carrying his voice up his nose, described the beauties of the piece, reassured us about its provenance, and kicked off the bidding as high as he dared. He was rarely disappointed; the crowd had obviously come with cash in hand, but I guessed that some of the wealthiest bidders were holding fire. They were waiting for what the auctioneer called, "the highlight of the evening: two splendid Picassos from the master's vintage periods."

With that buildup, I was thankful that I'd at least done them in oils. And they did look good, spotlighted tastefully against the dark velvet curtain. The whole process took the painting from the mess and smell of the studio with paint and wine bottles and cigarette butts underfoot, and in Picasso's case, children running about, not to mention the wives and models and lovers—in short, the whole muddle and uproar of a busy life—and turned it into Art with a capital *A*.

The auctioneer started at nine hundred pounds. This was impressive. I consider it a good day's work if one of my pictures sells anywhere near that price, but the weeping Dora Maar took off like a V-2 and didn't start to slow until she had made almost ten thousand pounds.

"Nine fifty. Do I hear ten? Ten thousand pounds. Thank you, sir. Ten, do I hear ten fifty? No, ten thousand pounds? Ten thousand pounds?" A slight pause, then he tapped the desk with his gavel. "Sold for ten thousand pounds."

By the time the evening was over, Hugo Kovar, formerly Samuel Goldfarber, had cleared the better part of eighteen thousand pounds sterling. The bastard had pulled it off, wherever he was, and I felt that I needed a stiff drink. Not at the depleted drinks table, either. I wanted a pub, preferably a seedy one, a little psychic chaser after the luxury and deception of the auction rooms, where I'd been entangled but good in a very professional fraud.

Before, I'd had fantasies of exposing Goldfarber. How about a telegram to Richard? *Goldfarber in London. Stop. At Claridge under name of Hugo Kovar. Stop. Fakes at Sotheby's. Stop.* I'd rather liked that idea before I saw how convincing the two "Picassos" looked. I'd have to prove the case, and it would be my word against the reclusive collector and the auction house. Confession in this matter might be good for the soul, but would be disastrous for my career and probably ineffective.

I'd also considered a little blackmail. I really did think I was owed something for damages after my time with the KGB, hence my visit to the Claridge and my calls to Mr. Kovar. Would I have been successful if Kovar had picked up the phone or accepted visitors? I'm not so sure. Perhaps I should have telegraphed the Tangier police commissioner, instead: *Goldfarber hiding Claridge Hotel, London. Stop. As Hugo Kovar. Stop. Selling paintings. Stop.*

That might still be the best plan, but if Goldfarber had any sense he'd be off somewhere without extradition before the commissioner could line up the London authorities. There was another serious complication: a lack of evidence. Thanks to Goldfarber's sharp eyes, there was now nothing to prove that those two expensive "Picassos" had come from my brush. And what were the odds that either Richard or Harry would back up my claim? Infinitesimal.

Goldfarber might lack finesse, but between him and Richard,

I'd been checkmated. At this dismal realization, I turned north toward Regents Park, away from my normal route home. It was an unexpectedly mild night and the city shine, reflecting off the low, cloudy gray sky, made walking pleasant. I have some happy memories of dark London parks during the early days of the blackout, and perhaps that is why I found myself heading toward those convenient groves and shrubberies. You never know whom you'll meet in the shadows, and during the war, certain young fellows almost reconciled me to the ever-dubious delights of nature.

So I was not alarmed when I heard footsteps behind me. The crowd had been leaving the auction rooms, and the tap of high heels rang along the sidewalks. These, however, were male and solitary, and they followed me from the post auction bustle. I didn't bother to look back until I entered the park, hung with mist and shadowed by its ancient trees. I remembered when the lawns had been dotted with bomb craters and heaped with bricks and rubble from destroyed buildings. Now with the walks and bridges repaired, the shattered trees removed, the ponds clean, the whole area was once again suitable for midnight encounters. I passed under a streetlight and turned to see a robust shape in a long coat and a bowler hat. Coming my way? I walked on but slower, for I was up for adventure.

Another look back told me that he was carrying a cane. Very Mayfair, indeed. I slowed down a little more, and when I reached the shadow of a convenient tree, I stepped off onto the grass. A moment later he was beside me, a large, powerful man whose face was shaded by the brim of his hat. I heard a click and realized that his walking stick was actually a long and gleaming sword cane. My heart jumped. There's always the chance of a mistake with these excursions. That's the point of the thing in a way, but there are moments when piquancy turns to terror.

A quick glance assured me that the park was deserted, and the traffic out on Baker and Marylebone sounded faint and sporadic. "Armed for all eventualities?" I asked. I'm happy to say that my voice seemed steady.

"For you, Herr Bacon," he said, and he lifted his head just enough so that I recognized him.

"You hardly need cold steel for me, Herr Goldfarber."

"Please. Hugo Kovar."

"That could be arranged," I said. "We could certainly agree on that."

He gave me a look. "What were you doing at the auction?"

"Admiring the works of the Spanish master. Unfortunately, they were too rich for my purse. Or I would certainly have bought them."

"Would you really? There's no need to worry, you know. They're as authentic as can be. We must be philosophical, Herr Bacon. There are many fine works by anonymous hands, including some that bear famous names. We have performed an artistic service, Herr Bacon, as certain lovely things that were destroyed are now resurrected."

"For your very great profit."

"Well, Herr Bacon, I could be generous, although you did owe me for the painting in Tangier, or I could kill you. Either presents problems." He made a face to indicate the difficulties of his position and the weight of his decision. What's in a name, asked Shakespeare; in Goldfarber's case, plenty. With the proprietor of the unlamented Tangier gallery, I'd have been dead already. Hugo Kovar, with his cashmere coat, his bowler hat, his sword cane, and a big load of mitteleuropean angst, was a slightly different item with a little more restraint. Or maybe just disinclined to ruin his fine clothes.

He lit a cigarette and started to smoke with his weapon tucked under his arm. "You're sort of a loose end," he said after a minute.

"You've got more than one. Neither the KGB nor MI6 can be very happy with you."

"Security services are forever. They are immortal enemies. You are—what is the phrase—a horse of a different color."

"Yet you've known where I live for some time. You must have guessed I'd be in touch."

"What do you mean?" There was a note of alarm in his voice that hadn't been there before. "What do you mean I know where you live?"

"Why, from the fat man, your detective. He's been snooping around, following me at night, turning up outside my flat like a lovelorn Romeo. He pretends to be on a divorce case, but I'm a damn unlikely divorce correspondent, don't you think?"

Goldfarber stepped a little away from me. Something had put the wind up him for sure. "I hired no detective." He threw away his cigarette and gripped the sword in a businesslike way. "Walk," he said and nodded toward the furry darkness of a grove.

I didn't move, gambling that he wouldn't dare attack me so close to a main road. Once well into the trees, though, all bets would be off. He gestured again with the sword, but I heard a sound, and maybe he did, too, for he turned his head toward the road. It was the creak and whirr of a cyclist nearby.

"*Schnell, schnell!*" Goldfarber cried, forgetting his English in his agitation, and he hit me across the back with the flat of the sword.

I was protected by my leather jacket, but he and his long weapon were between me and the exit from the park. I dodged away as Goldfarber raised the sword. I assumed he knew how to use it— East Europeans of my acquaintance had been big on swords, sabers, and foils—and I was wondering how long I could evade a determined attack when I saw that luck was with me. There was a light bobbing along the road, the cyclist approaching. Goldfarber thought it well to sheathe his cane.

Run or wait, Francis? Wait, maybe, for there was an oncoming car, too, its lights spearing down the dark park road. The car passed the cyclist, before its headlamps swept over us both so that Goldfarber was momentarily blinded. That was my chance, and I started a mad, blundering dash, my heartbeat juddering in my throat, my lungs closing up. I'd not been as calm as I'd thought, for I was running not for the street but for cover and darkness.

I heard Goldfarber shout before the squeal of brakes and the sound of car doors opening. Trouble for someone. When I saw two men leap from the black car and charge toward him, I dived into the nearest shrubbery and lay flat under the wet, leathery leaves of a rhododendron.

Sounds of a struggle. I lifted my head to see that Goldfarber had his sword unsheathed again and was slashing it back and forth in a dangerous way. One of his attackers screamed as the weapon raked his face, then the three of them formed one dark churning shape in the glare of the headlights, before I heard a shot. Goldfarber, hit or startled by this serious turn of events, dropped the cane and broke away. They were on him in a minute, and their speed and strength made me shrink further down into the damp and mossy ground. Had they noticed me?

I really hoped not, because after a brief struggle, they got Goldfarber's arms behind his back. He was kicking and shouting in three languages, before one person struck him across the back of the head and the other launched him toward the car. They were set to muscle him into the backseat, when a woman screamed, "No!"

Everyone, surprised, froze. Me, too; I'd forgotten the cyclist and not guessed that it was a woman. I had to crawl halfway out of the shrubs to see her. She had stopped, astride her bike, and she was aiming a pistol, which she held two handed. I hit the ground the instant before she pulled the trigger. Goldfarber was not so lucky.

He straightened up convulsively, crumpled into one of his attacker's arms, then slid onto the sidewalk.

The two men were shouting with anger and surprise, and one of them fired back once, twice. I flopped face-down to breathe up leaf mold and dust and spores and dirty water. The woman would be dead, and they'd want no witnesses. If they remembered seeing me, they'd surely come looking, and I crawled further into the shrubbery, backing noisily into gnarled stems and broken branches. I froze again, but now I could hear a third voice shouting and the angry blast of a car horn. I raised my head just enough to see two dark figures leap back into the car. It took off with a screech of rubber, leaving Goldfarber on the tarmac.

I waited until I could take a complete breath, then stood up. Goldfarber lay motionless, and the cyclist, not dead at all, was standing beside her fallen bike. She was gripping her right arm, which had turned dark from shoulder to elbow. As I watched, she began a half-stumbling, half-walking advance toward where he lay, and when she came farther into the cone of the street light, I recognized Edith Angleford.

"Mrs. Angleford," I called, for I could see that she was, if not seriously hurt, losing blood.

She looked up. She was still gripping the pistol in her right hand, but the wound in her arm would not allow her to raise it easily. "Mrs. Angleford, you've been shot. We need to stop the bleeding."

She staggered toward Goldfarber. "Is he dead?"

I went to check for a pulse in his neck. Then I saw the bullet hole in one temple and the mess of the exit wound on the other side. I nodded. "A lucky shot. How you missed all the others, I don't know."

"I'm the best shot in Morocco," she said. The pistol rattled on the sidewalk, and she sat down heavily. I knelt beside her and eased her jacket from her wounded arm. The bullet had torn across her bicep but missed her chest.

"We need a bandage. Are you wearing a slip?"

When she nodded, I lifted up her skirt and grabbed the white garment underneath. Fortunately, it was a half slip and easy to remove, because the fabric proved strong and difficult to tear. I folded it into a bandage and wrapped it tightly around her wound. "Press on it. We need to stop the bleeding."

She was chalk white and breathing quickly, but she said, "We need to get out of here."

I helped her to her feet. "And you need a doctor, the hospital."

She picked up the pistol and shook her head. "Help me to the bike."

Well, that was lunacy, but I wasn't going to argue with the best shot in Morocco if she had a weapon in hand. I picked up the bike and steadied it, but when she tried to grip the handlebars, she gave a little cry and nearly fainted. Nearly, but not quite, for she was able to keep a death grip on the pistol. Maybe Tony was right after all, and she really was a Medea.

"You'll have to pedal," she said.

"I haven't been on a bicycle in thirty years."

"Supposedly, you never forget." Still clutching her wound, she struggled to raise the pistol. "Get on. I'll sit behind."

I didn't stop to argue about this. Cars would be passing, and I was already up to my neck in a hanging offense. Public indecency or inebriation I could handle; homicide was a different matter. Before I could decide how likely we could cross the park unnoticed, I got onto the bike. Edith sat on the rack behind, and with a jolt and a wobble I stepped on the pedals.

You never forget, but you surely lose skill. We swayed one way and another, and twice I had to put a foot down on the tarmac to keep from tipping us both onto the ground. Edith Angleford revealed a surprisingly complex and unladylike vocabulary. The work was surprisingly heavy, too, and I had to put my whole body into each pedal stroke as we toiled across the park.

"Where are we going?" I asked, once I'd managed to get us rolling smoothly.

"I rent a flat in Camden Town. My landlady loaned me the bike, so I have to get it back."

"Oh, right, all the way to Camden Town. You'll have a mess of blood on the machine."

She poked me in the back with the pistol. "Just pedal."

Onward, Francis. We skidded off onto narrow walking paths whenever we saw car lights or spotted pedestrians, and I kept the bike's headlamp off, but that brought some problems of its own. More than once, I had to hit the brakes or make a sharp, unexpected turn. It was after one of these that Edith slumped against my back with a groan. She'd been wobbling on the seat behind me, which didn't make my job any easier, but now, though she straightened up again, I was afraid she was going to pass out. I didn't fancy wheeling an unconscious woman around the park, especially not with a murder weapon in the bike basket.

"You need a doctor," I said.

"A doctor will report to the police."

"Maybe not," I said, because I'd had an inspiration. At the first phone box I saw, I disregarded the pistol, braked, and pulled the bike over. "We need help," I said. "Of an unofficial nature."

Fortunately, she agreed with my diagnosis. She managed to get off the back, stood uncertainly for a moment, then sat down on the ground. I went into the phone box and tried every number I could think of for Freddy, a midlevel thug I'd met in the course of a wild night toward the end of the war. We'd stayed in touch. I was amused by his stories of criminal machinations, and he coveted one of my paintings. Whenever we met, we got along fine.

I'd run through most of my pocket change before I located him through a friend of a friend. Freddy was at a back-room poker game, and my call gave him a chance to take his winnings, so he was in a helpful mood.

"Francis! Long time!" For a man who spent his life in the shadows, literally and figuratively, Freddy had an emphatic speech pattern. "How're things?"

"Never better, personally, but listen, Freddy, I need a doctor fast."

"National health, now, old boy! You just go to the casualty ward and present your card."

"No can do on this one, Freddy. I need a doctor who operates after-hours, so to speak."

"I might know someone. Painful private ailment, is it? Or knocked-up lady friend—not that that's apt to be your problem." He laughed.

"Gunshot wound, Freddy, with blood loss."

"Why didn't you say?" And he gave me an address in Camden Town. "I'll call him! Get there fast!"

"Fast as I can. I'm cycling with the patient."

"Really, Francis!" he said in exasperation, as if I were the felon with a string of convictions as long as my arm, and he was the solid citizen. "You've got to learn to drive at some time!" And he hung up.

I helped Edith back onto the bike and resumed my labors. We came out of the park near the locks, and I said to Edith, "We need to lose that pistol. Can you think of a better place?"

"It was my father's," she said. "He carried it in the Great War."

"It will carry you to the gallows if you're found with it."

For a moment there was only the squeak of the seat, the click of the pedals, and the whirr of the derailleur. "All right, stop."

I did and she put the pistol in my hand. I pulled the bike close to the water, checked that there was no one around, and hurled the weapon into the canal. Then we resumed our journey, past the bridges with their dark abutments, past old stables and all the mysterious engineering of the locks, past tall warehouses, black with soot, and past the bomb ruins at their feet, overgrown with weeds and weedy shrubs, and under the railroad overpass with its rails and ties like a monster backbone.

To add to our joy, a drizzly rain came on, and we were both half-soaked before I reached Camden High Street. The doctor's house was off this on a narrow lane. His was a respectable, well-kept place with a light on in one of the upper rooms. I stopped the bike and steadied it so that Edith could get off. She was nearly dropping with blood loss and fatigue, and she had to hang on to the banister to keep from falling. I went up the steps and rang the doorbell.

A moment later, a light went on downstairs and the doctor appeared, a large bald man with a little goatish beard. He was wearing a white shirt with the sleeves rolled up and dark trousers and carpet slippers. His eyes were hidden behind lightly tinted glasses. "Don't stand about on the step. Come in quickly."

"The bicycle," Edith said.

"Leave it and help me get her inside," he told me.

She gave a little cry when he tried to help her along.

"Gunshot wound," I said. "Upper arm."

He led us down the hall and into his brightly lit surgery. "In here. Sit." He motioned toward a stout, well-padded chair. While I helped Edith off with her blouse and got her wrapped in a clean blanket, the doctor washed his hands. Then he brought over a tray of scalpels and needles and gauze pads and sat down on the stool next to his patient.

The doctor was well equipped. He had an examination table complete with stirrups, and I guessed that his specialty was illegal operations, but seemed competent for gunshots, as well. He cut away my improvised bandage, and dropped it, soaked with blood, in a kidney pan. In the bright light of the surgery, I saw that the bullet must have nicked one of the larger blood vessels.

Then he got to work cleaning the wound, preparatory to stitches and a proper bandage.

He hooked up a bottle of saline solution to Edith's other arm, and he gave her a shot of morphine. With this, she leaned back on the headrest, her dark eyes enormous in her bloodless face, and stopped trembling.

Even in her drugged stillness, Edith had an extraordinary face, one I must paint, and I wished for a photograph of her just at that moment, when she'd accomplished exactly what she'd set out to do and nearly lost her life in the process. How many of us can say the same?

"The bicycle," she said now, her voice just above a whisper. "Will you take it back? It goes in the shed at the end of the garden. The gate is never locked."

I looked at the doctor.

"You've got plenty of time to do that. She must have fluids, and the drip will take some hours," he said. "We'll need to keep her warm, too. She can't possibly leave in her present condition, and it will be safer for her to get a cab in the morning. Less noticeable."

"There will be a fee . . ."

"I have cash," Edith said. "You don't need to stay."

I saw there would be no escape from the Machine from Hell. I thanked the doctor, who grunted in acknowledgment. Out the door, onto the bike, which I must confess was a great deal easier to ride solo. By this time, the rain was pelting down, but I didn't mind that. Between the water falling from the sky and the puddles splashing up from the road, I was sure any telltale blood would be long gone before I returned the machine.

I was wet and miserable and an accessory to a capital crime. On the plus side, I'd lost a dangerous enemy, leaving only Goldfarber's "eternal enemies" to worry me.

One of them I would just have to avoid. I took care of the other the next morning, after I got home on the first train after the Underground opened.

I sent a telegram to Richard: *Goldfarber dead. Stop. Paintings sold. Stop.*

I signed it *Jerome Hume.*

CHAPTER SEVENTEEN

For some time, I expected a knock on the door, a not so friendly pair of detectives, and an invitation to assist with police inquiries. I knew that there had been people in the park, and I struggled to remember the dim shapes of drunks on the benches, of lovers under the trees, and of hopefuls along the shrubberies. And cars. Hadn't there been a couple of cars? They'd passed us at a distance, but still I opened the papers each morning with trepidation and turned to the crime news as eagerly as my old nan used to do.

Naturally, the Hugo Kovar killing was featured. *The Telegraph*'s article *Reclusive Collector Shot after Big Payday* will give you a feel of the headlines. The combination of serious money, a mysterious collector, and a violent death on the very night of a big glossy auction was almost irresistible. I was not surprised by the photos, by the police statements, or even by the speculations about Kovar and his relationship to the art market.

What surprised me was what was missing. Every morning and every afternoon and every evening, with every edition of every paper, I expected to read an appeal to "the cyclist seen riding through the park" or to "the man in the leather jacket seen in the vicinity" of Kovar's body.

So, although not exactly a nervous type, I turned daily to the Kovar story and its follow-up articles, convinced that I was going to be found out. *Couple Spotted on Bike Following Regent's Park Fatal Shooting*—that's the sort of thing I expected. Or *Witness Puts Mystery Man in Leather Jacket at Crime Scene.* But no. We got a request for information from members of the public who were in Regent's Park on the night in question, a vague appeal that was not going to bring too many folks out of the groves or from under the rhododendrons.

Indeed, for all intents and purposes, I was now better off, because my own private eye had taken a powder, met a terrible fate, or been called off the case. No more shadow near the end of our street. No more chubby silhouette at Tube entrances, no more footsteps ringing behind me in the night. I was on my own, and I was convinced that Goldfarber had lied. He'd hired the detective, and if I hadn't been alert and made the first move, I'd have come to grief one dark night. I was sure of it.

Just the same, I practiced a new and unwelcome caution. For weeks afterward, I walked on the inner side of sidewalks and was spooked by large, dark sedans. I even avoided some of my favorite locales at my favorite time of night, lest a large car roll up beside me and stocky, powerful men in bad suits pop out to grab me.

This was not a good frame of mind for yours truly, and I decided on a holiday to Cornwall, of all places. And of all the places in Cornwall, St. Ives, a so-called artists' colony, full of earnest landscape painters and daubers who traffic in local color and picturesque fishermen. Traffic in actual fishermen, I can quite see, but pictorially, never ever. It was the last place anyone who knew me would expect me to go, combining as it did the countryside, the beach, and a bunch of realists and/or abstractionists. It was, therefore, perfect.

I packed my kit, took some canvases, and promised my dealer that I would return with the goods in time for my show. I rented a cottage with a leaky roof that set off my asthma, and freed of the distraction of extra editions and aggressive newsboys, I buckled down to work. I had Muybridge's photos for inspiration, but I kept seeing a big, burly man in a good suit, and when I was finished with my wrestling men, I began to paint him. Dark against a midnight-blue ground and wearing a blue suit, he sat in some anonymous place. An airline terminal. A railroad lounge. A half-deserted bar. He had heavy features and black hair, and though I hadn't a photograph or any reference sketches, I knew that he was Goldfarber. That was all right; he owed me something. Definitely, he did.

I did several paintings of him. This was during the day. At night, I drank with the other painters, our artistic differences laid aside the minute we crossed the threshold of the local pub. Altogether it was a productive time. After six weeks, I got a carpenter to put together a shipping crate, and I sent my work up to London. My dealer was delighted; my show went well. It looked as if I had laid old demons to rest and was living a grown-up, sensible sort of life.

That couldn't last, could it? It may be, as Nan used to say, that some people can't stand prosperity. Maybe I am one of them, but I couldn't help thinking about Edith Angleford and wondering where she was and what would become of her. I hadn't heard from her, which was not surprising and smart under the circumstances.

I did go past her rented flat one day and noticed a FOR LET sign in the window, so she had gone and prudently, too, although the Hugo Kovar murder had long ceased to occupy the public prints.

But I'd been impressed with her devotion, and her example made me feel a little guilty, a little lacking. And then, I missed David, who rarely answered my letters, and the news I got about him from friends in the Zone was always scanty and never good. The day I got the first sales check from my gallery, I went straight to Thomas Cook's and bought a ticket to Tangier.

Up the Mountain in the velvet night, spring flowers blooming and a warm Mediterranean breeze. The American poet was leaning out the window of the cab to declaim his famous poem, which is very good in its own hysterical and hyperbolic way, hysterical and hyperbolic considering that most of the twentieth century's horrors had passed over him, personally, and over his fortunate country, generally. I didn't mention that, being fully occupied with the equally famous American novelist who is bending my ear about the "end of Tangier," by which he meant its upcoming incorporation into the Kingdom of Morocco and the end of the glorious Kingdom of Misrule, which had been his home for several years.

We were riding squeezed in beside my pal, the Moroccan painter, who was doing well enough now to import his own canvas and paints. He was with his mentor and patron, an older expat composer. The latter whistled a new tune, while the painter tapped out the rhythm on his knees and added little encouraging shouts and hoots, and everyone was merry except me. I'd gone straight from the airport to see David, a visit that had not gone well. I'd arrived with money in my pocket and thoughts of paying his debts and getting him on a plane for London.

He wanted no part of that plan. In retrospect, I'd been crazy to hope. When we first met, David had been rich and independent, while I had been, if not absolutely poor, subject to all the ups and downs of an irregular artistic income. Now he was relying on the piano bar to keep him in whiskey, while I was making good money off paintings he detested. I'd loved him, loved him still, but he only enjoyed my company when he could be in control and make me suffer.

And at that moment, everything in his life beyond the keyboard was out of control. So he was off to play the night away at the Meridian, and I was bound for the Mountain and a party given by my former acquaintance and maybe present enemy, Richard Alleyn. It should be an interesting evening.

We paid the cabbie and entered the pretty courtyard with lights glowing amid the trees and reflecting in the fountain. Inside the house, we were back in the old Tangier with most of the old crowd, with champagne and kef and *majoun* and brandy cocktails, with gossip and flirtation and politics. I kept an eye out for Harry from the consulate and MI6, but there was a different fellow representing Her Majesty. This one was also blond and fit and bland of feature; they must order them in bulk from Oxbridge.

I set up shop near the champagne tray, waved to old friends, and collected congratulations on my show, thus spreading as much cheer as I was able. I had almost reached a good alcohol level when I spotted Edith Angleford, and champagne-cushioned or not, I got a little shock. Sometimes when you are painting you sense that there is something wrong with the design, something you can't quite put your finger on. You turn the picture upside down or check it in a mirror or a Claude glass, and suddenly with the change in perspective, the error jumps out at you.

That's what I felt when I saw Edith Angleford. She was out of place, somehow, although she was well known in the Zone, although David had been friends with her late husband, although most of the foreign colony had come to his funeral. Just the same, I saw her, and I was suddenly as sober as I was likely to be. I made my way across the room to where she was standing, momentarily alone, examining one of Richard's paintings.

It was hung in a lighted alcove, and when she moved her head to see who was approaching, I saw that it was the Marie-Thérèse "Picasso" I'd done in emulsion.

"Hello, Mrs. Angleford." She was wearing a black cocktail dress with a low-cut neck but half sleeves to conceal what I guessed must be a nasty bullet scar. "How are you?"

"Mr. Bacon." She extended her hand, brown from the sun. The fingers were strong, but I could not help noticing that her arm was a trifle stiff.

"You have recovered," I said.

"After a fashion. I'm no longer the best shot in Morocco."

"I am sorry to hear that."

"It could have been worse." She took a sip of her drink. "But I never thanked you. If you didn't save my life, you certainly saved me from"—she groped for the right term—"real unpleasantness."

I thought that a murder charge could easily fall under that heading. "Thanks would have been indiscreet. Besides, if you hadn't come by on the bike, I might well have been skewered."

"Oh, yes. Goldfarber, Kovar, whatever his name, would surely have killed you. As quick as he killed Jonathan."

Her face tightened into a tragic mask. Although I was beginning to have my doubts about her, her passion was genuine. When she turned and walked down the hallway, I followed. She did not speak again until we had stepped out into the garden, where the smell of kef mingled with some sweet, night-blooming plant. The moon was big overhead, and we were momentarily alone.

"I only wonder why Goldfarber hadn't acted sooner. He'd had me followed, you know."

"Really?"

"Oh, yes. By a little fat private detective, surprisingly fast on his feet."

I saw her teeth white in the moonlight as she smiled for the first time. "Homer would be pleased you recognized his turn of foot."

"Homer? You know him?"

"I hired him."

"You hired a private detective to spy on me?" This put a different complexion on the whole affair. Goldfarber hadn't lied, and I guessed that the KGB had forgotten all about Jerome Hume.

"Sometimes the indirect approach is best," she said. Her voice was calm, without the brittle quality I'd detected inside. "I knew Goldfarber would contact you sooner or later."

"How did you know that?"

"You'd visited his 'studio'; you found Jonathan there. And you're a painter."

"No," I said, and I saw a quite different pattern. "The world is full of painters. You knew about Richard's scheme. You must have. And you must have known that Goldfarber was laundering money from the—"

She interrupted me. "Do not be indiscreet, Mr. Bacon. Not here."

"Your husband wasn't a double agent," I said. "He wasn't an agent at all."

"One of life's little annoyances is how rarely men listen to women. I told you at the start that Jonathan was an idealist. That he believed in Morocco, in Moroccans, in their independence."

"And you believed in other things and had other contacts." I understood now how she had gotten out of London, how certain lines of investigation had been neglected. "You were working for Richard all along. Keeping tabs on Moroccan organizations through your husband, I don't doubt."

There was an uncomfortable silence.

"I am responsible for his death," she said after a moment. Her voice was a mere whisper in the darkness, and for an instant I was unsure if she had really spoken. "They found out about my activities. Past activities, Mr. Bacon, not present. And not anything I can discuss. But Goldfarber and his contacts suspected Jonathan, though he was entirely innocent."

Entire innocence is not a concept I subscribe to, but allowing for exaggeration, I understood why she had been so distraught and so bent on revenge. "Did your husband know anything about your past 'activities'?"

"Not really. He didn't want to know. The war required so many compromises. He got out and wanted life to be straightforward black and white with no shades of gray."

"Some of us are strictly shades of gray," I said.

She nodded.

"They protected you in London. MI6 or whatever they're called there. They saw you got away."

"No, Mr. Bacon. *You* saw that I got away. And I'm grateful. Had we been stopped, you'd have been in serious trouble. And I suspect the only defense you could have mounted would have ruined your career."

"I only got you as far as the doctor's, and here you are, safe in Tangier with no sign of prosecution and in good odor with Her Majesty's spy corps."

"Our interests were momentarily aligned," she said calmly. "That does sometimes happen. They wanted Goldfarber."

"Why? Why did they want him?"

"You probably know that better than I do."

"But dead? If your husband was not working for MI6, revenge didn't come into it, did it?"

"You'd have to ask Richard. But wasn't Goldfarber already of interest to the police?"

Too right, which brought us to the murder of an earlier forger, my predecessor, the "Spanish boy," who was neither a boy nor Spanish. Though our acquaintance was limited to a couple of black-and-white police photos, he was the reason that I'd become entangled in Zone police matters and with not one, but two spy services. Possibly he, rather than Jonathan Angleford, had been working both sides, and it was his death, instead of Angleford's, that was crucial.

"You understand," she added in a more reflective tone, "a murder trial would not have been in anyone's interest. Grieving widows are effective on the stand and inclined to be reckless. I wouldn't have worried overmuch about the Official Secrets Act if I were on my way to the gallows."

"Gallows! Dear lady, don't speak of such things!" Richard exclaimed. He was standing silhouetted against the lights of the hallway with only the red tip of his cheroot lighting his face. For a large man, he was surprisingly soft-footed, and though his bantering tone suggested full party mode, I wondered how much of our conversation he'd overheard.

"And Francis, too." His voice chilled by several degrees.

I thought that he might throw me out, but Edith said, "I have reason to be grateful to Mr. Bacon. How strange life is, Richard. You know, I once threatened to shoot him." She raised her left undamaged arm to pat him on the shoulder, then walked into the house leaving us alone.

Richard drew on his cigar and blew out a cloud of smoke. We watched it eddy over the palms and mimosas and dissolve into the moonlight. "What are you doing here?" he asked in what I thought of as his official voice.

"Why, sampling the delights of Tangier."

"This is not a healthy place for you."

"Yet I have been impressed with the care you've taken of Mrs. Angleford. Even an amateur can see that someone fixed the case in London."

"Edith Angleford has deserved Her Majesty's gratitude."

"I feel slighted, Richard. I truly do. Surely Her Majesty hasn't been informed of my contributions."

"Some things, dear boy, are best left unsaid." He was silent for a moment. "Those paintings made some price in London."

"I was in the auction room. In spite of myself, I thought they looked impressive."

Richard gave a reflective, "Hmmm," and I remembered rumors that even his inheritance was hard-pressed to sustain these lavish parties.

"Don't even think about the one in the hallway. You don't have Goldfarber's skill. The provenances were ironclad. He had everything but Picasso's prints on the canvas, and if he'd been able to cut off one of the old man's fingers, he'd have had that, too. And he'd removed my initials. Yes, yes, I'd thought to protect myself, but he spotted them."

"There were two paintings in the auction," Richard said, almost too casually. "What happened to the other two?"

"Don't know. Goldfarber took three. One was left behind—unfinished and too wet to move. If Tony Coates, Mrs. Angleford's yachtsman, survived, maybe he took it. That's why he was there—he was going to sic Edith on me if he didn't get one. If he didn't make it or didn't get off the floor soon enough, there are other possibilities." I waited a beat and added, "I don't see Harry here tonight—or is that just a coincidence?"

"Officers are rotated regularly," Richard said stiffly. I thought there was a good chance that either Harry or Elena had made off with the almost finished Picasso. Too bad for Tony; he'd have to think of another way to pay off his debts on *The Aurora*.

"That leaves one 'somewhere in Europe,' as we used to say."

"I'd assume so, probably complete with provenance and appreciating in value every moment."

Richard gave me a sour look. "They were, of course, paid for by Her Majesty's Government."

"Not that *I* got anything out of it! Kindly remember that they were done under duress and without your Official Secrets Act and all the rest, I'd cheerfully tell the world."

"Your silence has been duly noted, as well as your assistance to Mrs. Angleford. But full-scale protection for you is simply not on. You have enemies here, and you'd do well to leave on the morning ferry."

He took a final draw on his cheroot and threw the butt into one of the flower beds. "Your usefulness to us is at an end," he said. "Keep that in mind."

CHAPTER EIGHTEEN

I did not take Richard's advice. I rented a small flat in Tangier and pretended that I was there to paint. What I really did was embark on a round of drinking and parties and beach boys as if bidding farewell to my youth. Maybe I was. Mine had lasted a lovely, long, irresponsible time, and let it never be said that I didn't give it a good send off.

I hung around the rougher parts of the medina at all hours and visited the sailors and smugglers' dives down by the harbor. Sorry to say, just about everyone I picked up was very far from "Mayfair" in every conceivable way. And David? David was drinking himself to death to a jazz beat, pounding the keys nightly at the Meridian, improvising on the thousand and one pop tunes he knew by heart like some latter-day Scheherazade. Only while she was courting the shah and having fun in bed, he was courting the grim reaper via single malts and Spanish brandy.

I stopped by his room almost daily. Note I say "room." The rather pretty house was long gone, the rent money having vanished into the pockets of a mob of thin, pretty, lamented boys and into the capacious wallet of the proprietor of the Meridian. Now David played for drinks, and how he covered his rent I have no idea. Sometimes the door stayed locked; other times, he'd let me take him to lunch.

We'd go to a cafe in the Petit Socco, both hung over and irritable. Sometimes he'd eat and rouse himself to be amusing, but more often he'd sulk over his wine or flirt with the waiter or proposition some passing youth. Even that was better than the days when he remained silent in his room, leading me to panicky imaginings of other, swifter exits from this life. I almost envied Edith Angleford, who'd had an enemy and gone after him without hesitation and could say she'd done all she could.

I avoided the Meridian. That is to say, I resolved every evening that I was never again going to set foot in the place. And almost every evening by eleven or so, I'd find myself with one group of friends or another who were going, definitely going, to the only place with decent jazz and a decent piano, the only place where one saw *tout* Tangier: the Meridian. In truth, I didn't want to go, and I couldn't stay away.

There were rare evenings when David was in a mellow mood. "Ah, Francis!" he'd call, as if he hadn't seen me in days, as if I had just arrived in the Zone, as if I were a longed-for and welcome companion. Then I'd sit beside him on the piano bench, matching his whiskey with champagne, and for an hour or so, it would be like old times, the good old times. "Pull yourself together, Francis!" Nan would say in my ear, but I ignored her, just as I ignored Richard's warning.

Of course, I took Richard even less seriously than I took Nan.

I ignored clear signs that someone was interested in me and not for my well-known charm and beauty. Footsteps behind me, dark cars in my vicinity? Sure, I noticed, and more than once I jumped into a cab and had it take me to the Palace Hotel, one of the Zone's clean, well-lighted places. There I took a room and stayed locked in it until morning, when I made a stealthy exit through the kitchens.

But I didn't book passage on the ferry to Gibraltar or appeal to my gallery for funds to fly home. There are times when safety just isn't the ticket, when internal weather of the heavy variety demands a bit of external bluster. Or in my case, the ever-piquant dangers and pleasures of rough trade.

You might say that at last I was really appreciating all Tangier had to offer, and it still offered a lot, despite the best efforts of the police commissioner and the prospect of the new Islamic monarchy. Yes, indeed. I was out every night, collecting bruises until near dawn, when I would leave a favorite dive near the beach. I can still hear the old Flamenco singer, a woman with a long, horsey face and a voice like a foghorn with secrets.

Then came a night when the moon was down, and a stiff sea wind raked the dark shore. I was quite drunk, which takes some doing because I have a great capacity for alcohol and a talent, let's face it, for self-preservation. Maybe I'd become infected with David's despair, or maybe I had already decided on a flamboyant end to a fool's errand, but instead of turning toward the town or caging a lift from a friend with a car, I walked down on the beach, strewn with weed and rubble and smelling of sewage.

What was I there for? A vague notion of adventure covers the ground, as I'd been eyeing a young fellow in the taverna. He wore a faded red turban and a loose shirt over canvas trousers, and his face was tanned almost black, although his eyes were a light, steely gray. He cut up his bread with a lethal-looking knife and knocked back glasses of red wine before singing the bass line along with the Flamenco artistes. I bought him a drink, and he courteously declined another as he was momentarily due on his ship.

Just the same, I left ahead of him and loitered along the shore—time's winged chariot and all that in the back of my mind. I expected him, you see, and I wasn't alarmed when I heard voices over the wind and turned to see two strangers approaching. In a sober frame of mind, I might have, would have, heard alarm bells. At the moment, full of crazy expectations and a powerful desire for oblivion, I raised my hand in greeting. Then I saw that the younger man was not my turbaned friend from the taverna. This one was short and broad-shouldered and wearing a bad suit. Inadequate tailoring has acquired a particularly sinister meaning for me, and when he threw down his cigarette, I recognized my danger. By then it was too late, for he was close enough to lunge at me, and my reflexes were not quick enough to evade him.

I landed full length onto the sand. I swung my fist at his face and squirmed from his grasp. I managed to get to my feet, but before I could make a run back toward the taverna, his companion struck me hard in the ribs. I fell onto the sand again, my face in the wrack and shells and stones. I got to my knees, swinging wildly, desperate to get upright and away from the flurry of blows and kicks that sent blood pouring from my nose and mouth.

I even held up my left wrist with my replacement gold watch, but these weren't robbers. They were set to beat me blind, and with a huge effort, I seized one of them around the knees and, unable to get onto my feet, sank my teeth into his thigh. A shout and then a blow to the back of my head. I had a split second to register extreme danger, then nothing more.

Wet, that was the first sensation. Something wet on my face. And then damp, to which add gritty and a sharp pain in my ribs that echoed one in my lower back. Then a brilliant light that closed my eyes and twisted up my features and caused a frightful pain in the back of my head and an irresistible desire to lose everything I'd eaten or drunk since first thing in the morning.

Voices in Berber, and I was lifted from the sand.

I automatically began to struggle before a voice said, "*Police. Vous êtes hors de danger maintenant.*" I felt a surprised relief, then I remembered nothing more.

I woke up with a headache, like the worst imaginable hangover. Add to that a nasty sense of impending nausea and the feeling that the bones of my torso had been rearranged in some infelicitous way. I wasn't breathing right, either, and a timid investigation of my nose revealed wads of cotton packing. Broken? I removed the packing, loosening crusts of blood that sent a nasty rivulet down the back of my throat and led to an acquaintance with the kidney-shaped pan beside my bed.

I was in the hospital. St. Barts? Guy's? Queen Mary's? Some unknown private clinic? That didn't seem right. St. Barts was in London. And I was . . . ? For a moment, I faced a fearful blank. I hadn't a clue and unwilling to guess, I closed my eyes.

The next time I woke up, I felt, if anything, worse, with a rich assortment of pains and scrapes and a thumping at the back of my head, which was wrapped up in a turban—no, in a bandage. There was a turban somewhere, although I couldn't locate it. But I wasn't in London. I knew that now. Which opened the interesting question of my location. Paris? Berkshire? Monte Carlo? No, something in the air was not right. Some smell, some spice, a little whiff of sewage.

And then I knew. I was in Tangier, and somehow I had gotten off the beach where I had been. Been doing what? Night, I'd been on the beach at night, expecting, anticipating—who? What? A man with a turban. For wild revelry with no more than a few bumps and bruises. I'd looked at the sea, that dark omnivorous void—*Stay away from beaches, Francis!*—and then . . . then, nothing. Until a bed, a hospital bed, a kidney-shaped pan, pain all over.

Had I picked up a psychopath? Had my sense for danger let me down? An unpalatable idea, and maybe it was just vanity, but I thought not. Not the man in the turban. Not him. Who? And the beach? Why the beach, which is no more than tolerable to me at best? And why that particular stretch of shore, which was filthy and abandoned?

A variety of ideas floated in and out of my mind, but, unable to concentrate, I went back to sleep. The next time I woke up was near sunset; outside I saw big shadows and the intense, saturated colors of North Africa. I was lying in a hospital with a drip in my arm, and I'd been beaten badly. Because I had walked on a beach where I never should have gone. For a moment, just for a moment, I understood David perfectly and knew that his beach was the Meridian.

"You must take the bitter with the sweet, Francis," Nan said in my ear. I was about to argue that point with her when the door opened.

In walked a smart police officer in a fine uniform. He had a thin face with a long jaw blue with stubble and large, black, dissatisfied eyes. He handled his cigarette elegantly, and he stood for a moment, smoking and looking me over. I got the impression that he didn't much like what he saw. Well, he wasn't at the top of my charts, either. I closed my eyes experimentally to see if I could evade him by dropping back into the nether regions, but this time I remained conscious. At least marginally. I opened my eyes again.

"You have suffered a head injury, monsieur."

I would have nodded, but I couldn't risk moving my head.

"You might well have been killed."

Although I don't trust policemen on principle, I believed that.

"Who?" I asked. My voice sounded weak and far away as if it intended to take a powder and leave me entirely. I cleared my throat and tried again. "Do you know who?"

"We have arrested two men."

"Two?" I tried to remember two men and failed.

"Can you tell me what you remember, monsieur?"

"The beach," I said. "I remember walking on the beach below the taverna."

"Alone?"

"Yes. But with good hopes."

His lips twitched with distaste, but he said nothing.

"Then I woke up here."

"You were attacked by two men. Both known to the police."

I had an image of a park, a big London park, and then of a small stone room. "Soviets?" I guessed.

But the officer had said all he was going to say. "It is unsafe for you here. You are to leave on the first ferry tomorrow."

I started to protest, but he held up his hand. "You will be given a ticket. Your safety here, monsieur, can no longer be guaranteed. And we lack the manpower to protect you on beaches below tavernas. *Bonsoir*, monsieur."

He made a little formal bow, turned on his heel, and strode out.

I lay still for a moment, making an inventory of my various aches and pains. I sat up experimentally. My head throbbed, but I stayed upright. Then I pivoted and tried putting my feet on the floor. The tiles seemed a long way down but after a moment, success. *Stand up, Francis.* That was a little less successful. I sat down again, aware of a tugging at my arm.

Of course, the IV line. I checked the bag. Almost empty. I picked away at the white sticking plaster and pulled out the needle.

Clothes, now. Where were mine? Pants on a chair. No underwear. Will have to do. No shirt. No jacket, either. Ruined with blood and vomit, probably. I struggled into my pants; even they were crusted with sand and dark spotted with blood. I tucked my long, open-backed hospital gown into the pants and looked around for shoes. Lost on the beach, probably.

I felt in my pocket and touched my wallet. Inside, I was surprised to find a handful of bills remaining. That gave me scope, and I immediately made plans to decamp. Secretly seemed best, and I opened the door to check the situation. Though I watched for several minutes, the ward must have been changing shifts, because I saw only one nurse, and she was far down the hallway. Just the same, I preferred not to risk the main entrance. I walked barefoot to a utility stairs that led down to the laundry room and went gingerly out into the hospital courtyard, trying to keep my throbbing head steady.

On the street, I hailed a cab to the souk, where I bought a cheap shirt, a large straw hat, and a pair of sandals. Did I say that I had a plan? In retrospect, nothing so sensible. So what was in my mind at the moment? One word: David.

I sat at the very back of a quiet cafe until dark. I drank mint tea and ate a handful of dates, unable to face anything more substantial or more alcoholic. Although I'd felt fine exiting the hospital and tolerable shopping in the souk, I was now barely upright. A visit to the cafe lavatory revealed a catalogue of damage, including one eye blackened and swollen shut. My nose had been permanently altered, and I'd lost a tooth. My head was wound with an impressive blood-stained bandage. "You should be in hospital, Francis," said Nan.

I had no intention of that. Eight o'clock. Nine o'clock. At nine thirty, I pushed back from the cafe table and moved slowly and stiffly through the evening crowds to the Meridian. I hesitated on the sidewalk, listening. When I heard the piano, I went inside.

Early yet for the Meridian crowd, but David was already playing. I recognized "When They Begin the Beguine," one of his favorites, and ignoring the surprised (and sometimes shocked) glances, even the occasional greeting, I made my way to the piano. A murmur followed me, and I suddenly hated the whole crowd. They knew our history, and they were expecting, hoping even, for a scene. Though many were amusing, and some were friends, I would not miss them. Not one.

I staggered against a table and came to rest leaning on the piano.

David looked up. "You've been in the war, Francis." It was a statement with neither surprise nor sorrow.

"Two men tried to kill me." I sat down on the bench.

"Well," he said without looking at me. He put a wealth of suggestion in that one word.

"Not what you think," I said. Meaning adventures, meaning rough trade, meaning smugglers' haunts and general recklessness—although the latter were indeed implicated.

He took a drink. I noticed the vast number of empty glasses adorning the top of the piano. "You should not have come back," he said in a dull, affectless voice. "You are not safe here."

"I couldn't stay away. Though I wanted to."

David did not respond. I had the sense that he was far away, that he had succeeded in leaving our ordinary life behind. He began another tune, "The Man I Love." He laid out the theme, then buried the melody in variations and chromatic wanderings that escaped my comprehension. "Consider me dead, Francis," he said.

They picked me up outside the Meridian. Two spiffy policemen with a car. I didn't resist. They drove me to the station, where, to my surprise, they didn't put me in a cell. I was led, instead, to what must have been a sort of break room with a quite comfortable cot. I was locked in, just the same, and one of the officers in careful English told me that I was to "leave on the morning ferry." He also asked me for the keys to my room and said that my bag would be delivered in time.

So I had all the comforts and service of a decent hotel, courtesy of the Zone police, and in the morning, I had a visit from the top man himself, who intended to escort me personally to the ferry. Had I not felt half-dead, I would have had questions about the whole proceeding, but preoccupied as I was with my unhappy body, I consumed the roll and coffee I was offered and got meekly into the big black Chevy that served as the commissioner's personal chariot.

We were early for the ferry departure, and the commissioner had his driver park along the waterfront and take a cigarette break.

When we were alone in the car, the commissioner said, "You understand, monsieur, that you must leave? And stay out of Tangier?"

"What I realize is that this is all illegal."

"There is a certain legal flexibility in the Zone," the commissioner agreed.

"Then there is nothing to stop me from refusing to leave."

There was a silence. "Very soon, we will be incorporated into the Kingdom of Morocco. I would like to present the new authorities with a good record for protecting the safety of our inhabitants and visitors. When one is in danger, it is my job to do my best to protect him."

I said nothing to this. The man was beginning to sound reasonable.

"You do not like me," he observed. "Because I am a *colon*, a *pied noir* from Algeria with a provincial French accent."

"Wrong. I dislike policemen in general. You are only a particular instance."

"I am immensely reassured. Yet, monsieur, I am what passes in the Zone for an honest man. By which I mean that, if a man works usefully for me, I do not betray him and I do not seek to harm him when his usefulness has ended."

Even in my altered state, I felt a chill at that echo of Richard's parting comment: *your usefulness to us is at an end.* I had imagined that was just a figure of speech, just Richard's usual desire for a flourish. Maybe not.

"Not everyone in authority around here can say the same," he continued. "Indeed, they dare not."

I took a breath, but my voice still sounded hoarse as I struggled to recalibrate all my assumptions. "I had thought the Soviets to blame. They tried to grab Goldfarber in London."

"The late Herr Goldfarber was a big fish, a tunny, eh? Worth their effort. You, monsieur, are one of the minnows. They must eventually have realized that."

"Would they had realized it sooner," I said, my mind racing. "You know, they wanted to pass me off to Moscow as a top spy from London."

"There are mediocrities in every profession," he said and shrugged. "But do you understand what I have told you? I cannot be more specific."

"Yes. Although I am taken aback, Commissioner, I believe you. But what possible motive?"

"I am not privy to the activities of your legation—or its various auxiliaries. Money and power are always good bets, though."

"I lean toward money," I said after a moment. "There were two paintings sold very profitably in London. One is still presumably in Europe. The other was left in the protectorate."

"Paintings by the famous Picasso?"

"Let us say, paintings 'after the famous Picasso.'"

He lifted his shoulders. "And someone took this last picture and wants to sell it safely?"

"Something like that. Or else sheer meanness."

"Ah, monsieur, never underestimate that."

"I misjudged you, Commissioner. I must thank you."

"Well, monsieur, I believe only in necessary meanness. I owed you for your efforts with Herr Goldfarber." He rolled down the window and waved to his driver. He said nothing more until he wished me bon voyage at the ferry ramp.

I went on board, full of troubling speculations about Richard and Harry. I remembered Richard's false bonhomie and his chilly voice, and Harry's careless arrangements for my safety and his outright lies. I remembered the parties and the gaiety, but also Richard's avid greed for art. Yes, I believed the commissioner. I was not safe here, where Richard was an important figure. And London?

London, I thought would be all right; the rules were different there, I hoped, and our situations would be different. There, I was an up-and-coming painter and Richard was a provincial secret agent away in far-off Tangier. Besides, I was only a threat to him here, where he aspired to be a leading light in Tangierino society. Yes, I was a London man and London was the ticket for me, first and last.

With that in mind, I let my attention stray to a picturesque ferryman, as young and muscular as a Greek bronze. I watched him unfastening the hawser and thought about what pigments would best capture the planes of his naked back. I did not look toward the shore again until we were pulling away from the dock, and the turbulent, dirty city was once again a beautiful white illusion, gleaming against the dark edge of the continent. For a moment, I thought I saw David standing on the crowded dock, and my heart in my mouth, I stood up and waved.

But it was not him at all, just a trick of the light, just his ghost, who I fear will haunt me now wherever I go.

THE FRANCIS BACON MYSTERIES

FROM MYSTERIOUSPRESS.COM
AND OPEN ROAD MEDIA

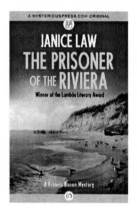

Available wherever ebooks are sold

MYSTERIOUSPRESS.COM

OPEN ROAD
INTEGRATED MEDIA

MYSTERIOUSPRESS.COM

Otto Penzler, owner of the Mysterious Bookshop in Manhattan, founded the Mysterious Press in 1975. Penzler quickly became known for his outstanding selection of mystery, crime, and suspense books, both from his imprint and in his store. The imprint was devoted to printing the best books in these genres, using fine paper and top dust-jacket artists, as well as offering many limited, signed editions.

Now the Mysterious Press has gone digital, publishing ebooks through **MysteriousPress.com**.

MysteriousPress.com offers readers essential noir and suspense fiction, hard-boiled crime novels, and the latest thrillers from both debut authors and mystery masters. Discover classics and new voices, all from one legendary source.

FIND OUT MORE AT

WWW.MYSTERIOUSPRESS.COM

FOLLOW US:

@emysteries and Facebook.com/MysteriousPressCom

MysteriousPress.com is one of a select group of publishing partners of Open Road Integrated Media, Inc.

THE MYSTERIOUS BOOKSHOP, founded in 1979, is located in Manhattan's Tribeca neighborhood. It is the oldest and largest mystery-specialty bookstore in America.

The shop stocks the finest selection of new mystery hardcovers, paperbacks, and periodicals. It also features a superb collection of signed modern first editions, rare and collectable works, and Sherlock Holmes titles. The bookshop issues a free monthly newsletter highlighting its book clubs, new releases, events, and recently acquired books.

58 Warren Street
info@mysteriousbookshop.com
(212) 587-1011
Monday through Saturday
11:00 a.m. to 7:00 p.m.

FIND OUT MORE AT:

www.mysteriousbookshop.com

FOLLOW US:

@TheMysterious and Facebook.com/MysteriousBookshop

CPSIA information can be obtained at www.ICGtesting.com
Printed in the USA
BVOW05s1031030914

365348BV00005B/337/P